# Musings

## of a

# Writer

**The complete collection**

# Stacey Broadbent

# Musings

## of a

# Writer

The complete collection

Dedicated to

the Ashburton Writers' Group.

Thank you for always challenging me. This
collection came together because of you.

# Contents

**Fear of the Unknown**



**Laughter is the Best Medicine**

# Introduction

I'LL START by including this little piece I wrote as an instant exercise with the Ashburton Writers' Group. The prompt was "My life was boring until…" and though my life wasn't boring, it certainly has changed for the better since joining this group.

My life was boring until I joined Writers' Group and met this crazy bunch of women who encourage and inspire. I was a nervous wreck that first day, as I'd been asked to come along and talk about myself. Public speaking is not my idea of fun (though since then, I have been invited to speak at other events), and I was petrified. What would these people be like? Were they normal, easy-going individuals like me, or were they intellectual scholars who would talk above my head? I had no clue what to expect.

Walking into the room, I was instantly set at ease as Rae offered a warm smile while Debbie and Julie regaled us with tales of their weekend. That was when I knew I'd found my people, and life, quite frankly, hasn't been the same since.

It's because of this group that these stories and poems even came about. Aside from my books, I hadn't attempted poetry or short stories since I was in high school, and I have to say, it really challenged me. But in saying that, I believe some of these are my best stories – and many are only 500 words long! It's because of this I've decided to release a collection of *Musings, Mournings, and Misadventures*. I want to share some of my favourites, and perhaps invoke a love of short stories and poems in you, the reader.

At the end of each story, I've included a little bit to tell you where the inspiration came from; most of which were prompts from our monthly assignments at Writers' Group.

I hope you enjoy this collection, and if you enjoy writing and want to challenge yourself, I encourage you to seek out your local writing groups.

Much love!

Stacey xxx

# Musings of a Writer

Stories and poems about nothing and everything.

# Books Abound

THE MINUTE I step foot over the threshold, I'm hit with the intoxicating smell of wisdom and years-old paper. My eyes take in the myriad of tables stacked in the stadium, each one filled with books of all shapes and sizes. My heart races and my breath quickens as I try to decide where to start. Do I go straight for the specials table, or try my luck among the throngs of people crowding down the aisles of older paperbacks? Do I peruse the biographies, or see if I can find something humorous to read? So many choices, and not enough hours to examine each and every piece! What's a girl to do?

I liken it to an alcoholic staring at a fully stocked bar. This intense craving to own all the books takes over my body, and I can't stop myself from adding more and more to the bag until it's filled to the brim. And what's worse, I know I'll be back for more. You see, this is my favourite week of the year. Bookarama comes but once a year, and with the excuse that the money goes back into the community, I put aside the need to pay bills and let loose, buying everything my heart desires. I know I'm fighting a losing battle in finding time to read all my purchases, but this does not dissuade me from making more. In fact, I find myself making bargains with myself, promising that this year I'll get through more of them.

Time goes by so quickly when you're in your happy place, and before I know it, it's time to head back home. If I'm quick, I can make it before hubby walks in and sees me in my drunken stupor, surrounded by books. I know I've only got mere minutes to get them inside and hidden away, but even so, I'm drawn to have just one last look at the table nearest the door. My fingers trail along the spines, caressing the words that sing to me until I force myself to avert my eyes and take a step back. I have to be strong. I have to get home.

With my arms full of my purchases, I quickly run up the steps to my front door, fumbling with the keys. Beads of sweat trickle down my forehead at the rush of adrenaline coursing through my veins. I'm going to get away with it! If I could just get down to the bedroom without—

"What's in the bag?" Hubby leans against the doorframe, his arms folded across his chest and a smirk on his face.

"Uh… nothing?" I edge sideways, trying to squeeze both me and the bags of books between hubby and the door. He turns in, taking hold of one of the bags. "It's not what it looks like."

"Oh? You mean it's not a bag of books from Bookarama?"

"Um…" I look down at the overflowing bag in my arms. No amount of talking is going to get me out of this. Not when the evidence is right there between us. I've been caught red-handed again.

*Every year, the Rotary Club of Ashburton holds a Bookarama – one of my favourite things! And every single time, I go in there several times during the week and come out with more and more books, even though I already have shelves full of books and a kindle full of ebooks! The addiction is real, people!*

# The Eighth Day

If I had an extra day,

Do you know what I would do?

I'd sit down with a cup of tea

And a pack of biscuits too.

I'd curl up in my comfy spot

And grab my favourite book.

I'd read from start to finish

In my cosy little nook.

I'd take my time and appreciate

Each and every letter.

I can tell you now, by the end of the day,

I'd be feeling better.

You see, reading is my happy place,

Where I can be a different me.

So if I had an extra day to use,

That's where I would be.

# The Burial

I STOOD BY THE GRAVESITE. We were burying Uncle Eric – again. It was hard enough the first time, back before they recovered his body, but this was so much worse. More final.

Almost a year ago to the day, we'd held a funeral, burying a box containing only his picture. He'd been missing for six months by that stage, and it was all we could do to move on with our lives.

Six months is a long time to live in a constant state of worry. Every time there was a knock on the door, a deep sense of dread would settle in the pit of my stomach, wondering if this would be the police informing me of his whereabouts. That call never came. Not until recently.

Eighteen months after his disappearance, they found his decimated remains in a secluded spot, miles from our home. I guess in the back of my mind, I'd still been holding on to hope that he would turn up unscathed, so when they dropped that bombshell on me, I fell to my knees, sobbing, knowing there was no way he could've got that far on his own. He was ninety-three and couldn't walk more than a few steps without his walker, and even then, it was slow going. He rarely left the house, and never on his own, so when I woke up that morning and found his bed empty, I knew something wasn't right. I'd driven the streets, searching everywhere I could think of to no avail. The police had put a call out, and they'd been thorough in their investigation, but no one thought to look that far afield. Poor Uncle Eric died all alone, in a ramshackle cabin in the middle of nowhere.

Watching them lower his casket, I was filled with the what ifs. What if I'd gotten up and checked on him during the night? What if I'd been out earlier, scouring the streets? Questions filled my mind, drowning out my sorry as I sought a way to shoulder the blame for something I had no control over.

"You can't blame yourself." A wrinkled hand came to rest on my forearm as Barry stepped in close, a sad smile on his face.

"I don't," I lied, patting his hand.

"I can see it in your eyes. The blame will eat you up, if you let it. Take it from an old man, it's not your fault."

My eyes filled with tears. "But—"

"No buts about it. Here." He bent down with a grunt, grabbing a handful of dirt and placing it in my hand. "Take this. Put all your guilt and anger inside, and let it go." He scooped another handful, holding his hand over the casket. He closed his eyes, whispering something I couldn't hear before opening his fingers and letting the dirt fall through to the casket below. Turning back to me, he said, "Your turn."

So, I did as he said. I focused all my hurt, anger and guilt into that pile of dirt in my hands, then whispered a goodbye as I let it go.

A weight lifted off my shoulders that day, as I said goodbye to Uncle Eric for the last time.

*This was a tough one. Our prompt was to write about burying Uncle Eric again, and it took me quite a while and several rewrites to get this one down. My instant thought was to use humour, but no matter how many times I tried, I just couldn't quite get there. Instead, I ended up with a sad tale of regrets and forgiveness. It's not what I planned, but I'm pleased with it all the same.*

# A Thing of Beauty

Tell me, what's your favourite thing to see?
She asked me on a sigh.
Well that depends on many things,
was my quick reply.

On a cold and stormy day,
I'll find beauty in the rain,
I'll watch it forming patterns
as it slides down my windowpane.

But then the sun will come out
and a new thing I will find.
It could be something small
like the eyes of someone kind.

There's beauty all around us
if we only stop and take a look.
You might find it hidden
in the pages of a book.

So, keep your eyes wide open
as through the years you will grow older,
And remember, beauty is always found
in the eyes of the beholder.

*I struggled with this one at first. I had messaged one of the other members, saying how I couldn't think of anything to write, and she quickly listed some prompts about the weather, scenery, or a song to dance to. It was the fact that she'd listed so many different things that can be beautiful that I thought, I'd turn it into a poem about just that – finding the beauty in everything.*

# Second Chances

AS I CRAWL ON HANDS AND KNEES across the broken shards of glass covering the pavement just so I can lick up what I can, I realise this is what rock bottom looks like. Jobless, homeless, and no one to call out to for help. It's no wonder I turned to the only true friend I have left; a bottle of Jack.

I know what people think of me. I see it in their eyes as they shuffle past me on the street, trying hard not to look at me so I don't ask for money. My scruffy clothes and dishevelled hair disgust them, as does the fact I'm normally sitting here with a brown paper bag to my lips. They know it's not water I'm drinking. They know, but they don't care enough to reach out. It's much easier to sit on your high horse and look down on others, than it is to stop and offer a hand to those in need. It makes them feel important.

I used to be important. Maybe not to everyone, but to my friend, Tobin, I was important, at least for a while. Back before it happened, and everything changed.

We'd been best friends since preschool. Our houses were on the same block, and we would play in the streets together almost every day. I was a bit of a tomboy back then, and we spent a lot of time climbing trees and exploring. People often mistook us for boyfriend and girlfriend, but it was never like that. We were just the best of friends. Tobin wasn't much of a talker, but he was a great listener. He'd sit there nodding his head while I babbled on about anything I felt like. He was the one person I knew I could trust with my secrets. Unfortunately, he didn't feel the same way about me.

We were thirteen when I first noticed his mood swings. He could get angry at the drop of a hat, and then with the snap of a finger, he'd jolt out of it, wrap a smile on his face, and pretend that everything was fine. I think back now and wish I'd reached out more, made him realise I could be a good listener too.

It was 3am one autumn morning when I knew. I'd woken from a terrible dream and couldn't shake the feeling something bad had happened. I nearly wore the carpet bare from all my pacing as I waited for Tobin to respond to my text. He never did.

Fourteen, and the only boy I'd ever wanted in my life was gone. It felt as though my soul had been ripped from my body, and I couldn't breathe anymore.

That was when Jack and I became acquainted. I remember sneaking swigs of the amber liquid when my parents weren't looking after the funeral. It helped to ease the noise inside, helped me to forget the pain. It was a poor substitute, but as long as I had Jack, I had a friend on my side.

Throughout the years, it picked me up when I was down, quietened my inhibitions, and took away the pain I fought against every damn day. The pain that I wasn't able to help my friend when he needed me most. That he suffered in silence for God knows how long, and never felt like he could tell me. It might not be a physical pain that others can see, but it's there all the same, always lingering and reminding me. *I* know it's there, even if no one else can see it. That's the beauty of Jack, though. I don't have to pretend anymore, because it takes over my mind for me, pushing away the thoughts that threaten to pull me down. With Jack, I can be 'normal' like everyone else.

By the age of sixteen, I was consuming a bottle during the weekdays just to get by, and more in the weekends. I found a nip each morning helped me ward off the desperate thoughts until I could make it home for another. I would lift money from my parents every chance I got, and I took to using a five-finger discount on a regular basis. I did whatever I could to keep me and Jack together. I got pretty good at hiding it too. As far as my parents and teachers were concerned, I was coping just fine; a normal, stand up student. Not even my friends knew just how much I was drinking back then. Not a single soul.

Over the years, though, I became sloppy. It became harder and harder to hide my addiction, and even harder to quiet the noise. Jack isn't quite as good at keeping it at bay anymore, so I've had to increase my intake a touch. I'm on my third DIC conviction, I lost my car, my license, my job, and now, my apartment. My 'friends' turned against me after the first, saying I wasn't who they thought I was, and it was time to grow up. But they didn't understand the war I fought each day. The one that made me feel older than my years. The war that made me feel *everything* on a grander scale than most and made it impossible to function sometimes. They didn't understand that I *needed* Jack to keep me sane so I didn't end up following Tobin.

Just one more sip and then I'll be good. I don't know how many times I told myself that over the years, but it never quite sunk in. One would turn into two, then three, then before I knew it, I was waking up on the sidewalk with my dress hitched around my waist, wondering what the hell happened.

Broke and alone, watching the world go by as if I'm merely a bystander. I've lost count of the days; it doesn't really matter when you've nowhere to be and no one to miss you. One day rolls into another, and I don't know whether to be thankful I survived another night, or resentful I didn't leave this place to meet Tobin.

A door across the street swings open and music blares out from the bar as two men stumble out. One lights a cigarette while the other dons a thick jacket that looks cosy and warm. I pull my knees into my chest a little tighter.

The one with the cigarette hanging from his lips sees me first. His head swivels in an exaggerated double take as he takes in my dishevelled appearance. I don't need a mirror to know my hair is a tangle of knots and my clothes are caked in mud. I stretch the thin fabric of my dress further down my legs in hopes of covering more of me from his sight. Something about the way he watches me has the hairs on the back of my neck standing on edge and shivers racing down my spine.

"Hey, you!" he yells, already crossing the empty street towards me. I push my back against the concrete wall behind me, hoping that somehow, it'll open and take me into its depths. Anything would be better than what this man has in store for me. His hands fumble with his belt buckle as he looks left and right before coming to stand before me.

His mate shuffles from foot to foot across the road, his hand scrubbing through his short-cropped hair. "Come on, man. Leave her alone," he calls, and an uneasy dread settles in the pit of my stomach.

"Nah, man. I'm gonna have me some fun." He grabs his crotch, sucking his lip between his teeth as he looks me up and down. "Wanna have some fun, baby?"

I pull my knees in further and drop my chin to rest atop them. Maybe if I pretend he's not here, he'll leave me alone. The thought is futile, but I cling to it anyway. I know from experience, it's easier to go to that far off place in my mind and let him do his bidding than to fight.

His heavy black boot kicks my shin, making my eyes water, but still I don't engage.

"Oi, bitch, I'm talking to you. Didn't your mama teach you no manners?"

"Jarod, stop. Leave her alone."

"Or what?" Jarod spits, and I hear the unmistakable sound of a zipper before my arm is wrenched up and I'm dragged around the corner where it's dark.

I close my eyes and let my body go limp, conjuring up the last happy memory I have of Tobin. We're riding our bikes across the school grounds on a warmish autumn day. His head is tipped back, and the sun shines on his face, giving him an ethereal glow. He's never looked more perfect to me than in this very moment. I hold on to that perfection as my dress is pushed roughly aside. I bask in the sounds of leaves rustling mixed with his laughter as my legs are spread apart and my knickers torn from my body. I watch us race across the field, the wind whipping through our hair. I go so deep into my memory; I don't feel anything but bliss. It's almost as if I'm really there with Tobin, and I wonder if perhaps I am. If perhaps this time my tormentor took it too far and I've finally joined my best friend in the afterlife.

"Get off her!" a voice cries out, jolting me from my blissful dreams. I blink once, twice, my eyes adjusting to the dark surrounding me. A trash can crashes to the ground above my head, and I quickly sit up, yanking my dress back down to cover me. Pressing my back against the wall once more, I watch the scuffle between Jarod and his friend, my saviour. My body shivers from adrenaline or the cold, I'm not sure. For the first time in a long while, I wish I was back home with my parents. Back where I had a roof over my head and food on the table. Where I felt safe from random men who thought they had the right to my body. But how can I go back now? I can't show up on their doorstep and expect they'll take me in with open arms. Not after everything I put them through.

"Miss? Are you okay?" My saviour stumbles towards me, leaving Jarod lying in a heap on the ground. "Miss?" I flinch away from his outstretched hand, and he stops, turning his hand up. "Woah there. I'm not going to hurt you." He nods his head at the pile of flesh behind him. "I'm sorry about him. He can be a jerk when he's had a few too many. He's never done anything like this before, though." He takes another cautious step forward. "I didn't mean to scare you, I just had to make him stop."

My eyes flick between him and his friend and back again.

"Did he hurt you?"

It takes a minute for my brain to register the question, and I honestly have no idea of the answer. "I… I don't think so." My fingers press into my flesh, searching for any bruises.

"What about… um…" He nods his head towards my lower half. "Are you okay? Can I take you to a hospital?"

"No." I shake my head, wrapping my arms around my legs to make myself as small as possible. "I'm fine. I'll be fine."

"Hey." With his hands still up in the air, he crouches down, his eyes never leaving mine. "I promise I'm not going to hurt you. I just want to

make sure you're okay. It's the least I can do after…"
His voice trails off as he waves his hand behind him.
"I really am sorry."

"Why do you keep doing that?"

"Doing what?"

"Apologising for him. It's not your fault he's a jerk."

He chuckles, ducking his head to his chest. "No, I suppose it's not. Guilty by association? I don't know." He shakes his head before holding his hand out to me. "I'm Daniel."

I eye his hand before reaching out and taking hold. "Mia." His skin is softer than I expected, and it hits me how long it's been since I've touched someone. Really touched them. It's nice, comforting almost.

"You hungry, Mia? I was thinking of grabbing a bite to eat."

My stomach rumbles at the mention of food, but there's no way I can accept his offer. "I'm not really dressed for public consumption." I pull at my tatty dress with a snort. "You go, though. You don't have to worry about me. I've been living on the streets a while now. I can take care of myself."

"Well, see that's where you're wrong. I'm involved now, so I will worry. I'm just going to grab a pie down the road, nothing fancy. Here." He shrugs out of his jacket and hands it to me. "You can wear this."

"Oh, I can't take your jacket."

"Sure you can. It's easy." He smiles as he gets to his feet and offers his hand. "Ready?"

His jacket does look warm, and it would be nice to have a full stomach for a change. I take his hand, and he pulls me to my feet. Pushing my arms through the sleeves of the jacket, I sigh as I'm engulfed in a warmth I haven't felt in a long time. So used to the cold, hard concrete walls and a threadbare dress, I revel in the luxury. Daniel takes my hand again, leading me down the road, and once again I notice how pleasant it feels to be touched. Have I really fallen so far I've lost touch with humanity altogether?

"If you don't mind my asking, how long have you been living like this?" Daniel's voice is quiet and thoughtful, so unlike anyone else who encounters me. Most walk by without even a second glance, and the rest treat me like a piece of garbage under their shoe. In fact, I don't think anyone has really stopped to talk to me since I became a permanent resident of the streets. I'm generally given a wide berth. I guess people think homelessness is contagious.

"The days all blend into one out here. I don't really know how long it's been." I tilt my head up to meet his gaze. "Long enough to forget there are still kind people out there."

"We're out there. You just have to know where to look." He winks, and we continue walking. It's bizarre how comfortable I feel with Daniel. There's no awkward silence I feel I need to fill, just a comfortable quiet.

"Mia?"

"Mmmm?"

"Will you let me help you?" He stops, taking both my hands in his. "I can't bear the thought of leaving you on the side of the road where some other bastard can force himself on you."

I reach a hand up to cup his cheek as tears fill my eyes. "It's not your fault Jarod did what he did, Daniel. It's sweet you want to help, but you don't need to save me. It's not on you." I step back, waving a hand down my length. "I did this to myself."

He shakes his head. "No. You can't tell me you asked for this life. I don't know what happened for you to wind up here, and I know I can't change it, but I *can* help you get back on your feet. Everyone deserves a second chance, Mia." He fumbles in his back pocket, bringing out a leather wallet. "I can help you, you just have to say the word." He hands me a card with a bird in flight at the top. Below that are the words *Second Chances* and his name.

"What is this?" I ask, flipping the card over. "You're like some saving grace or something?" Fresh tears fill my eyes as hope blossoms in my chest. After so much disappointment in my life, it's a feeling I've not allowed myself to acknowledge, but the genuine look in Daniel's eyes has me right there with him, feeling it.

He chuckles. "I guess you could call it something like that." He turns back to the path, his hand falling to my lower back as he ushers me forward. "Come on, let's get in out of the cold." He points to a building ahead that boasts *coffee at any hour of the day.* I hesitate at the door, still unsure if I'll be welcome, but Daniel assures me everything will be okay.

"Daniel!" the waitress calls out as we enter, and he gives her a wave before leading me to a booth down the back.

"On a first-name basis? You must come here often." I quirk a brow at him as I take a seat, shuffling across to lean against the wall.

He holds his hands out. "What can I say? They make great pies."

"What can I get you two, doll?" the waitress asks, popping gum and pulling a pencil out from behind her ear.

"You trust me?" he asks, and I nod. "Two beef, egg and potato please, Dharma."

"You got it. Any coffee?" Daniel looks to me before nodding, then she toddles off to the kitchen.

"So, Second Chances?" I ask, clasping my hands on the table. "You roam the streets searching for women to save?"

He smiles and his eyes light up. "It's not quite as simple as that, but that's the general idea, yeah." Leaning back in his seat, he continues, "My mother was a drug addict. I grew up on the streets, scrounging for food, huddling under awnings for shelter. When I was seven, she was caught propositioning an officer, and I was taken into a group home. It's the first time I remember having a real roof over my head and a proper meal."

"What happened to your mother?"

His face drops and he scrubs a hand across his jaw. "Still on the streets. I've tried to get her clean, but she fights me every step of the way. Sadly, some people don't want to be helped, and she's one of them."

"So you turned your powers of good to other women on the streets?"

"Pretty much. I know how hard it can be to get out once you're in that situation. I offer a way out to those who *want* my help. It breaks my heart that there are people out there who feel like they have nowhere to go and no chances left in life. I count myself as one of the lucky ones." It all sounds too good to be true. No one is *that* nice.

"And you want to help me?" I watch my finger draw circles on the table between us, not able to meet his gaze as I ask my next question. He seems like a decent guy, and what he's doing is noble, but I know from experience, people can be deceiving. Everyone is out to help themselves. "What do I have to do… in return?"

He rears back as if I've slapped him. "Nothing," he whispers. "You don't have to do a damn thing in return. Not for me, not ever." I slowly lift my eyes to meet his and see nothing but sincerity staring back at me. "I promise you. I will never hurt you, Mia."

Two steaming coffees and pies are placed in front of us, then Dharma leaves just as discreetly as she arrived. My mouth salivates at the delicious scents, but I wait until Daniel picks up his fork and begins eating before I dig in. I may not have much left in the way of dignity, but I've still got my manners.

That first bite is like heaven, and I swear I can hear angels sing as I chew and savour the buttery pastry filled with chunks of meat and gooey cheese. If this is what second chances taste like, I want it. "This might just be the best thing I've ever put in my mouth." I let my head fall back against the chair as I take another mouthful.

Daniel holds his fork in the air in a salute. "Told you. Best pies in town." He smiles, watching me eat the first real food I've had in days. "So, do you believe in second chances?"

Tilting my head, I purse my lips as I think for a moment. "You know, I think I just might."

*This story was meant to be for an anthology on inspiration, but I ended up going down a different route (humour), so it never got finished until recently when I decided to put this book together.*
*I think even though it wasn't used for the anthology, it's still a story of inspiration and hope. Unfortunately, we live in a world where people like Mia exist, making ends meet on the streets, and I wanted to show that there are good people out there who will stop and offer a hand to those in need.*

# Tomorrow is a New Day

When money is so tight
That you worry how you'll pay,
Just smile and remember,
Tomorrow is a new day.

When you're up at night with fevers
And you want to go to bed,
Just smile and remember,
You have a roof over your head.

When you sleep through your alarm
And you're late for work again,
Just smile and remember,
There's no rainbow without rain.

When there are deadlines at your back
And you feel you're out of time,
Just smile and remember,
You're actually doing fine.

When everything goes wrong
And nothing goes your way,
Just smile and remember,
Tomorrow is a new day.

*I like to think of myself as a positive person who tries to look on the bright side, but sometimes life can throw you curve balls, and it can be easy to tumble down a tunnel of despair. I know how hard it can be when bills are on top of you, and when you feel like there aren't enough hours in the day, so I thought I'd turn it into a positive reminder that things will be okay, because tomorrow is a new day.*

# Double Life

I'M LIVING A DOUBLE LIFE.

To my friends and family, I'm a wife and mother. I have a full-time job that I'm good at, and spend my weekends giving back to the community. I volunteer at every school event I can, and I'm a dab hand with a crafting knife and some glue. I am a pillar of strength.

But, behind closed doors, when the world has gone quiet and I'm left to my own devices, I'm none of those things. I'm a shell. An empty vessel waiting to be filled with something of substance. I spend my waking hours showing the world how together I am, how giving and nurturing I can be, when deep down, I'm lost. My life is nothing more than a visage. A portrayal of what I think I'm meant to be; the perfect wife, the loving mother, the friend you can count on. I give so much of myself to others, to prove this point and keep up the pretence, that there's nothing left for me. Nothing left to grip onto and steer me out of the abyss. The darkness that threatens to envelop me each and every time I close my eyes. Its gnarled fingers beckon me, enticing me to a world without pain and fear. A world where I don't have to be perfect, I just have to be me.

But can that ever truly exist? A world with no judgement or expectations?

It's in our very nature to judge the actions of ourselves and our peers, and I find it hard to believe that doesn't follow us through to the afterlife. But even with that thought in the back of my mind, the temptation is still there. The promise of an end and also a beginning. The path to a new start, free from the shackles of this earthly body.

Those gnarled fingers take hold, encircling my wrist and dragging me down to a place I can never return from. They whisper words of salvation while pulling me to their depths until my chest restricts and I feel as though I'm drowning in a sea of nothing.

And then I blink; once, twice, waking to face another day. My children greet me with smiles so serene, so pure. Unaware of the wars that waged inside my head all night, or how close I came to my demise in the throes of darkness, they wrap their little arms around me and squeeze tight, giving me something else to cling to. A power so strong it can reach into the darkness of my soul and eradicate the fear. A love that gives me strength to fight another day. To fight for my children, because to them I am *their* shining beacon, the light that draws *them* from the dark. I am the thwarter of boogeymen under the bed, the finger that wipes away their tears, the one who has the power to kiss a booboo and make everything okay again. I am the cookie baker, the smile waiting at the school gate, the arms that protect them from the world. I show them that there is always a way, and tomorrow *always* brings a new day.

I'm living a double life.

But that's just it. I'm living.

*This one was written for a competition in the Sunday News.*

*A dear friend of mine had shared her experiences with depression not long before I wrote this. She, and many of my friends, have had these feelings of despair at times throughout their lives, and though the path can be difficult, they've each fought their way back to where they're okay. For that, I am thankful.*

*I wanted to write something that shows the struggle of depression and anxiety, but also shows the guiding light that is there if we search for it and are willing to accept it.*

# Partners in Crime

"IF WE GET ARRESTED, it's your fault." I sling my bag over my shoulder and follow begrudgingly as Peter climbs the fence. The memory of old man Vickers in a red-faced rage when we were thirteen and caught playing in one of his sheds flashes before my eyes, and I quickly scurry to catch up.

"Pfft, you know we're not going to be arrested." Peter rolls his eyes. "You're so dramatic sometimes, Paige."

"You call it dramatic, I call it cautious. You know the thrill of being naughty is only good if you don't get caught." The snap of a branch echoes across the field. "What was that?" I crouch low, my heart pounding as I search for the culprit. I can't get caught again.

"Uh, it was you, you big galoot." Peter points behind me at the broken piece of wood under my foot.

I breathe out a sigh of relief. "Oh, oops. Didn't see that there." Chuckling, I climb to my feet and brush myself off. Peter trudges forward again, the abandoned cottage and our destination in his sights. "Are you sure about this?"

"Stop being such a chicken. It'll be fine. We're just going to look around, that's all."

"That's what you said last time, remember?" I look at him pointedly. "I thought for sure old man Vickers was going to have a heart attack, he was so red in the face." I shake my head, running my fingers through my hair. "You know I can't get in trouble again." My voice is quiet as I blink away the tears.

"Hey." Peter tilts my head to meet his gaze, his lips brushing against mine. "You're not going to get in trouble, I promise."

My hands fall to his chest, the fabric bunching in my grasp. "You don't understand, Peter. If my parents find out we've been sneaking around again, they'll stop us seeing each other." I blink up at him, my eyes flicking between his. "I don't want to lose you. You're my safety net."

His hand slides into the hair at the base of my neck as he presses his forehead to mine with a smile. "I'm not going anywhere." He takes my hand, giving a gentle tug. "Now, come on."

With a sigh, I reluctantly follow. Peter climbs the steps, stamping his feet. He looks back at me with a wink before pushing the door open.

"Surprise!" a chorus of voices ring out as I step through the door and the room lights up. Everyone I love stands before me with faces beaming. A large banner with the words *Happy Birthday Paige* hangs from the ceiling.

My vision clouds with tears of joy. "You did this?" I turn to Peter, and he nods.

"I had a little help." He cocks his head to the side and my parents step out.

"Happy birthday, darling," Mum says, leaning in to kiss my cheek.

I pull back, a frown creasing my face. "I don't understand."

Peter takes my hand and pulls me to the side. "I knew all the sneaking around was upsetting you, so I went to see your parents. We came to an understanding."

I quirk my brow, waiting for him to elaborate. There's no way my parents just allowed this without any fallback. They've had it in for him ever since we were thirteen and caught. The thrill has kept us together all these years.

"Peter, what did you do?" I whisper, my eyes wide.

"He's coming to work with me down at the station, where I can keep an eye on him. Isn't that right, son?" My dad claps a hand on Peter's shoulder.

"Yes, sir," Peter says, his eyes pleading with mine. "No more getting in trouble."

I plaster a smile across my face. "That's great, Peter." I excuse myself and make my way outside for some air. My heart thuds in my chest as I brace my hands on the railing and look up at the sky.

"What's the birthday girl doing out here by herself?" the familiar voice of boy-next-door, Ricki, asks from behind.

I turn to him with a devilish grin, linking my arms through his. "Hey, you know that old shed about a mile down the road? You wanna go check it out?"

*I'm a sucker for a good plot twist, and I knew straight away that Paige was going to be the real instigator of shenanigans and not Peter.*

*Not your typical story where the girl goes after the bad boy, but rather the other way around. Paige turns the good, wholesome boys into bad boys, getting that thrill she craves while she's at it.*

*One of our writers' group members is brilliant at giving us twists we don't see coming, and it's become somewhat of a challenge for me to try and do the same!*

# The year that tried to break me

2020 WAS MEANT TO BE MY YEAR. It was the year I was going to accomplish great things and reach the goals I'd been striving so long to achieve. Apparently, 2020 didn't get the memo.

It started off as I intended; weight loss, fitness improving, crossing things off my ever-growing to-do list… and then my account got hacked. Minor issue. Inconsequential even. But that was merely the tip of the iceberg in the year that was trying to crush my soul.

I've always thought of myself as a positive person. Someone who can find the light in the darkness and move forward. So, I did what needed to be done then carried on with my plans of world domination.

2020 had other ideas in store for me.

We had a death in the family right as the world was thrown into a global crisis, and something I never thought I'd see in my lifetime happened. We went into a full lockdown. Isolated. No socialising. Each of us pacing the house like caged lions as we watched the newsreels in horror. Wages were cut and job security was up in the air. It was a testing time for many, myself included, but I tried to remain positive and took the time to find myself again and enjoy my family.

When we were finally allowed out again, I was all set to go forth with my new goals and decisions, and then I lost the diamond to my engagement ring. A few days later, our shower began to leak. Then our family holiday to Australia was cancelled. No big deal. That's what insurance is for, right?

2020 laughed in my face.

I turned my attention to my work, trying to forge forward and get noticed, only to be met with rejection. I'm ashamed to say 2020 almost won. I may have taken a moment or two to wallow in self-pity and question my goals in life at this point. But after a kind word from my husband and some friends, I pulled up my big-girl panties and pushed on through.

We booked a family trip to Christchurch to give the children a semblance of a holiday. We woke the first morning to find ants had ransacked the kitchen and taken up residence in our muffins for the next day. The breakers went out and the heater in the bathroom began to smoke. And all the attractions we went to see were not as we had hoped. Such is life.

And then, as if that wasn't enough, on our way home, the car broke down. Well, that's not entirely accurate; my seatbelt broke halfway between

Ashburton and Christchurch, and all I could do was hope we didn't crash.

Within a few weeks of our return, our washing machine decided to pack it in too, and we had to use the last of our savings to buy a new one. The savings that was meant to get us overseas for another adventure when the world calmed down. That was my one lifeline I was holding onto through everything, and I finally had to admit defeat and call off another planned holiday.

That was another of those moments where I let myself wallow for just a little while, allowing the devastation of the year that was meant to be mine take over for a breath. Just a breath. No more.

After breaking down in front of my family, I decided to take action. 2020 could try its damndest to break me, but it would never succeed. I refused to let it.

I started listening to an audio book and began implementing small steps to get us back on track to having those much sought after holidays away. I began regularly exercising again to get those endorphins pumping through my body. I took action and sought help with my poor sleep, and it actually worked. I reached out to friends and family and told them how much I was struggling with this year and discovered I was not alone in my plight.

Bit by bit, piece by piece, I slowly put my life back together. I took charge and made the changes necessary to be happy. I took on 2020, and I won.

*The Year That Tried to Break Me* was written as part of an assignment entitled "and then the car broke down". I had been struggling to come up with a story to fit until we were on our way home from a family holiday and my seatbelt fell off. After a crazy year of ups and downs, emphasis on the downs, this piece kind of poured out of me when I got back home.
2020 was one hell of a year.

# A King's Demand

"ARE YOU SURE ABOUT THIS?" Egbert asked, a frown marring his round face. "It seems awfully unsafe."

"Oh yes, sir. It's what his majesty requested." The page boy nodded his head, his floppy hair bouncing up and down.

"But it's so... high." Egbert gulped, sweat forming underneath his hat. "Perhaps there is another way? Something not quite so... towering." His eyes searched the horizon for another solution. Preferably one that wouldn't have him falling to his death.

"There is nowhere else. His majesty is adamant. The show must go on, and that is to be your stage." He bowed his head, backing away before Egbert could say anything. "I'll leave you to your rehearsals."

Egbert sighed. "Very well then. If it must be, it must be." He tipped his head back to take in the wall he'd have to mount at King Leopold's behest. He couldn't fathom why his majesty would insist on such a feat, but then again, he had always had a thing for theatrics. Even as a child, Leopold had taken great pleasure in announcing to anyone who'd listen that he was next in line for the throne, and everyone was expected to fall to their knees and kiss his outstretched hand.

But this? This seemed a step too far. Egbert wasn't made for such things. His skin was not as thick as the king's, and heights scared the bejesus out of him. His hands grew clammy just thinking about it.

As the day wore on, Egbert became more and more agitated, knowing he was running out of time. Donning his Sunday best, he went over his notes one last time before resigning himself to his fate. There was no choice. He would have to climb the wall.

With knees knocking together and hands slippery with sweat, he slowly made his way to the tippy top. His eyes went in and out of focus as he made the mistake of looking down, and he dropped to his hands and knees, clinging on for dear life.

"Come on, Egbert, we haven't got all night! Tell me a joke!" the king taunted from his makeshift throne.

"Ah, did you hear the one about the, ah..." He gulped, closing his eyes as he tried to stop the world from spinning. A whoosh of air flew from his lungs as he pushed himself upright just a little too far, and then he was falling, down, down, down until, crack! His outer shell split down the middle and yolk seeped in a trail down his forehead. The audience gasped, some even clapped, unsure if it was part of the show. Why else would an egg be perched so precariously if it wasn't all a big act?

A nurse pushed her way through, dropping to his side and pulling a slice of bread from her handbag. She mopped up the yolk, taking a hefty bite. "Don't worry, Egbert," she said around her mouthful. "You're in safe hands." Then she slapped a 'handle with care' sticker on the side of his head and whistled for the ambulance.

*A King's Demand was written for an assignment entitled, "Handle with Care". Every time I thought of something fragile, an egg came to mind, and so I used the old nursery rhyme about Humpty Dumpty as my basis.*

# Shadow for the Day

Come and be my shadow,
If only for a day.
Follow in my footsteps,
And hear the things I say.
Up with the sun each morning,
And off out for a walk.
It's the perfect time for thinking;
There's no need to talk.

Now it's time for breakfast;
A piece of toast is fine.
Then drop the children off at school,
Watch them join the line.
Head off to the office,
Where messages await.
A manuscript to edit;
I'm up to chapter eight.

Working through the lunch break;
I need to push on through.
Another job is waiting;
In three days it is due.
Stopping for a coffee,
I open Photoshop.

I need to make some cute adverts
To make my pages pop.

Lost inside a rabbit hole
Of images and memes.
I can't decide which one to choose,
And I'm about to scream.
I scroll until my eyes do blur;
The pictures look the same.
How is one supposed to know
Which one will end in fame?

And then I must remember
To find some time to write,
That pesky little story,
That keeps me up at night.
Opening the file,
I wish for inspiration.
My brain of course refuses;
I've no imagination.

Closing down the laptop,
I heave a hefty sigh.
I'll leave it for tomorrow.
At least I gave a try.
The day is almost over,
And look what I've achieved;
No ending for my story.
No cover to be sleeved.

*This was an assignment from my early days in the group, with the prompt Shadow for the Day. I literally take you on a journey of a typical day in my life – where I can don the hat of mother, editor, author, cover designer, and housewife.*

# Scintillating

I WATCH AS THEY PARADE about in their garish costumes and masks, each one pretending to be something they're not. It's all just a ruse, a game they play to see who will stumble first. Who will crumble when push comes to shove. These parties are all the same; wheeling and dealing under the cover of darkness, everyone tripping over each other to come out on top. I'm only here as a talisman, a reminder of the secrets they strive to hide. And there are many. I have something over every single one of them, and when the time comes, I'll call on them to do my bidding in exchange for those secrets disappearing.

Lifting my whiskey to my lips, I scan the room for the one person who eludes me. The woman in the red dress. The one I know is lurking in the shadows somewhere, who clearly doesn't belong in a shithole like this.

I caught the briefest of glimpses of her as I stalked through the doors earlier this evening, a man on a mission that, in the wake of her distracting beauty, now seems futile. Sebastian is no fool, and he was smart to avoid attending the event that has been the talk of the underground for the last month. Little does he know, I don't give up easily, and when I want something, I get it by any means necessary. He'll keep. And until then, I will bide my time with the captivating woman whose locks of ebony hair curl down to her arse. She is by far the most scintillating creature I've ever seen, and I've had my fair share of women. There's something to be said about a woman so sure of herself she sees no need to be centre stage, clawing her way to the spotlight like all those other broads in their barely-there dresses and sky-high heels. One by one they'll all topple, and she'll be the one left standing. With any luck, she'll be by my side. Like I said, I always get what I want. And what I want, is the woman in the red dress.

Scintillating *was an assignment where we had to open the dictionary and point to a random word and then define it. My word was scintillating, but instead of defining it, I ended up using it in a story. I was inspired by a series of stories I'd read for an anthology where many wealthy people were attending a ball.*

# Home is...

Home is a place to rest your weary head;
An old leather couch, a soft, warm bed.
It's a place to relax and just be you,
To never be judged for the things that you do.

Home is a place held deep in your heart,
A feeling, a memory, and that's just the start.
It's a place filled with comfort, with feelings of glee,
The only place you're ever truly happy.

Home is the place where love feeds your soul,
It fills you up and makes you feel whole.
For a home, you see, is as simple as this;
Wherever your heart is, that's where home is.

*Home is... was written for the Wham Bam Author Jam limited edition anthology, No Place Like Home. We each had to write a poem or short story inspired by the word 'home'.*

# Less than Glamorous

"YOUR MUM IS SO LUCKY. I can't believe she gets to wear pretty dresses to work every night." My fingers trailed the silky fabrics hanging on the racks. I'd never seen so many beautiful outfits in one place before. Certainly not in my mother's wardrobe. She wore business suits to work, not slinky dresses. It made me wonder what Katie's mum did for a living. I'd bet it was something glamorous, like a model.

Pulling out a gold dress that crinkled, I held it against my body, imagining what it would feel like to wear. Never in my nine years of life had I seen something so exquisite. "I think this one is my favourite."

"Try it on. I bet it'll look rad on you."

My mouth gaped open. "You're allowed to wear them?"

"Uh-huh." Katie nodded, dragging a blue leopard print dress off the hanger and plastering it to her figure. She sucked in her cheeks and posed in front of the mirror, turning this way and that. "She doesn't care what I do. I do it all the time."

My eyes turned back to the dress in my hands. It *would* be fun to try it on, just this once. Who knew when I'd get the chance to wear something so gorgeous again? "Are you sure she won't mind?"

"Honestly, she won't care. She probably won't even notice. I mean, look at them all." She waved her arm at the bulging wardrobe. "I could take one and she wouldn't even know." She shrugged, swiping some bright red lipstick from the dresser and slathering it on. "I bet you can't guess what I had for lunch today," she said as she undressed. Of all my friends, Katie was the most confident. She wasn't uncomfortable like I was when I had to undress in front of others. Swimming days were the worst.

"Whatever it was, I bet it was nicer than my peanut butter sandwiches," I said as I gripped the dress between my chin and chest in an attempt to keep her from seeing my tummy as I pulled my clothes off.

"I had a packet of jelly crystals. Cool, eh?"

I frowned. "That's it?" My stomach grumbled in protest. Jelly crystals were delicious, but they weren't enough to fill you up so you could concentrate on work.

"Yeah. There wasn't anything else in the cupboard. Mum hasn't been to the shops again." She shrugged, but this time I noticed the sadness behind her smile.

"Maybe she's at the shops now," I suggested, stepping into the gold dress that suddenly felt less than glamorous.

"Nah, it's Friday. She'll be at work. Friday and Saturday are her best nights." She turned her back to me, lifting her hair from her shoulders. "Zip me up?"

Standing beside her in the mirror, I could see how different we looked. The shimmery fabric clung to my stomach, accentuating the rolls, while the leopard print hung off her small frame. For the first time, it occurred to me that perhaps her life wasn't as comfortable as mine. That maybe it wasn't the first time my friend had gone to school with an empty stomach.

Suddenly those extra rolls around my middle I'd been so worried about didn't seem quite so bad anymore. At least I knew that when I went home there would be a hot meal waiting for me and parents there to hug me, which was more than I could say for Katie in this cold, quiet house.

I always thought my life was ordinary and boring, but perhaps that's the truly glamorous way to live.

Less Than Glamorous *was an assignment based on the word glamorous. I instantly knew what I wanted to write about as this is a story based around my childhood. I have since tried to find my childhood friend, but to no avail.*

# The Dancer

Hushed voices, darkened room
Curling nice and small.
Almost there, nearly time
Trundling down the hall.
Door opens, shouts abound
Laughter off the wall.
Wheels squeak, music blares
It's my curtain call.
Lid lifts, bursting forth
Time to bare it all.
Bikini clad, heels strapped on
Feeling six feet tall.
Cheers erupt, clapping hands
Confetti starts to fall.
Hips gyrating, body shaking
On the floor I crawl.
Raining money, making bank
Collecting quite a haul.
Happy birthday, Mr. Man
I hope you have a ball.

The Dancer *was written as part of an assignment entitled "write about an incident that could be used against you if you ever ran for political office". It took me a while to come up with this one, as I kept drawing a blank. I finally decided to go with an exotic dancer turned politician as it always seems to be some sort of sordid/sexual activity that they get caught up in. I pictured the dancer leaping out of one of those birthday cakes and entertaining the guests.*

# The Writer

Weaving magic with only words,
A writer's voice can be heard,
Turning phrases to describe,
All the world seen from their eyes.

Painting pictures you can see,
Drawing from a memory.
Images of childhood fun,
Of finding faith; seeing the sun.

What you see inside your head,
Is but an image they have led,
With perfectly descriptive prose,
So you can see what they propose.

And that, dear reader, you will find,
Is what pushes the writer's mind.
For an author's voice needs only this;
To send their reader into bliss.

The writer *was another assignment. This one was to simply write a poem, and as it was a writing assignment, I felt it appropriate to use that as my muse. I'm really enjoying getting back into poetry. It's something I dabbled with as a child and young adult, and up until joining Ashburton Writers' Group, I've rediscovered my love for them.*

# What are Words?

THE CURSOR BLINKS TAUNTINGLY.
*No idea.*
*No idea.*
*No idea.*
It's been four hours of staring at the flickering screen with not an ounce of inspiration. Not one single word or even a lone letter has filled that gap. Only a blank page with that damn blinking cursor; a constant reminder of how far I still have to go.

I shift my gaze to the calendar on the wall with the large red circle around June 12th. I have... I raise my eyes to the ceiling, counting... seven days, five hours, and sixteen minutes to upload my manuscript to the editor, and I'm no closer than I was a month ago.

Fifty thousand words doesn't sound like a lot in the grand scheme of things, not when the first ten thousand flowed out with ease. The remaining forty thousand, however, that's about as daunting as it can get when you're staring at the abyss of writer's block.

Almost six thousand words per day, that's how much I need to write to meet the deadline, but it may as well be a million with the way I'm feeling. Under normal circumstances, I could knock it out in my sleep, but when Mandy walked out three weeks ago, she took my inspiration along with her. My muse, my light, the very reason I put pen to paper in the first place. Without her, the words won't flow. They've dried up like an over-used watering hole in the desert.

My fingers twitch, hovering above the keys I know so well, eager to work. Tentatively, I let them rest in place, the tiny nodules of the F and J keys beneath my index fingers like a beacon welcoming me home. Still the cursor blinks.

*No idea.*

*No idea.*

*No idea.*

Closing my eyes, I tilt my head skyward, searching for divine inspiration. The story is in there somewhere, I know it is. Locked away in the recesses of my mind, waiting for me to find the key. I pick up my phone, swiping the screen until my number one procrastination tool pops open and I begin to scroll. Friends from all over the world dance and chat and mime, occupying my mind and numbing the burning need to finish what I started. When I finally glance up, another half an hour has gone by with no words written.

Pushing my phone aside, I shake out my fingers, twist my head side-to-side, and turn my eyes to the blank screen once more. There's something there. A tiny niggling thought trying to push its way through, and I reach for it, grasping it tightly in my fist before it can run off again. My fingers glide across the keys, one word after another forming before my eyes.

I lean back, breathing a sigh of relief, for this surely can mean only one thing; the dreaded writer's block is no more. I have a sentence. One beautifully eloquent sentence.

The timer goes off, and with a triumphant whoop, I ease the lid of my laptop closed, giving it a loving tap before sliding it into the case. My allotted writing time is up, and though I'm only a fraction closer to my deadline, I can't help but feel a sense of achievement. Today, I did something I've struggled to do in weeks. I got words down.

*What are Words was written for a competition with the theme "A hard day's work" and a word limit of 1500. Even though I've worked in factories and retail, there's still nothing quite like staring at a blank page and knowing you've got nothing to add. It can be draining and disheartening, and that's why I chose to write about it. Writing is hard work, and it's made harder by our self-imposed goals and deadlines. Sometimes, you have to take the wins where you can, even if it means only writing one sentence.*

# 2032

The year is 2032, and haven't we come far?
Petrol prices hiked too high to fuel our flying cars.

We can't remember numbers or how to use a map,
Who needs to know that anyway? It's all found in an
app.

Our watches tell us when to sleep or how far we have
been
Our lives depend immensely on that of the machines.

No longer can we function using basic common
skills,
Instead, we need the internet to pay all of our bills.

Children don't know how to search for facts using a
book,
They never learned the struggle of the time it took to
look.

The world is at our fingertips, but still we want for
more,
Everything's too easy, and life is such a bore.

Yes, the year is 2032, and still we have not learned,
That so much more has meaning when you feel that it
is earned.

*2032 was an assignment with the prompt of 2032. I had a lot of fun with this one, picturing a futuristic life based on how things seem to be going in the world today. Covid has certainly changed things up a bit for us, but not as much as the use of technology and machines.*

# Autumn Daze

Pink cheeks, cold nose,
Breath puffing out like mist.
Hands tucked in pockets,
Fingers in a fist.

Beanie pulled down over ears,
Scarf around the neck.
Thick socks, warm boots;
Everything in check.

Leaves of orange and of red,
Crunching beneath feet.
Trees no longer dressed in green;
Their clothes spread like a sheet.

Hews of gold and amber,
The sky darkens to grey.
Quickened steps, down the path,
On this chilly autumn day.

Up ahead a library glows
With warm lights through the pane,
And scattered all about the place
Are books to feed the brain.

Scarf and hat discarded,
Curled upon a corner chair,
Descending into fantasy;
A land so far from here.

Escape the chill of autumn breeze
Inside a book of spring,
Where flowers bloom, the sky is blue,
And birds begin to sing.

While outside it gets colder,
The sun no longer high,
A world between the pages
Makes the time go by.

And when the journey's over,
The last page turned to close,
Scarf and hat are donned again,
Cool air tickling the nose.

Head tucked against the wind,
Back down the path once more,
Through the gate and up the steps,
Rushing through the door.

Home sweet home, or so they say,
Though I have to disagree.
The library with all its books
Is where I'd rather be.

*Unlike most of the stories and poems in this collection, this one didn't come from an assignment or competition prompt. I had been struggling to write for some time, and so I asked my daughter to give me a prompt. As soon as she suggested 'autumn', I instantly pictured leaves crunching and curling up with a book, thus Autumn Daze was born.*

# Atlantis

*Through the veil of the sea, the city of Atlantis waits
for me.
She holds her secrets to her chest, her treasures
hidden beneath the depths.*

DEEP GREEN WAVES crashed against the hull of
The Rose, rocking it gently as it journeyed across the
large stretch of water. With the sun just kissing the
horizon, the ocean had an almost ethereal glow.
Ahead, a jagged rock face jutted out from the middle
of nowhere, and Cezarne Peters could just make out
the tiny cluster of islands to its left. Lowering her
looking glass, she nodded to Bilkins. "I see it." The
first point to the triangle.

Dartanian Foxworthy turned his ruddy face to
her with a toothy grin. "Told you I'd find it." His
fingers curled around the rail of the bow, pulling at
the bindings on his wrist. It didn't seem to bother him
as he leaned forward, turning his face skyward.

"Your cockiness is unbecoming, boy."

The taunt hit its mark, and Dartanian stepped
his bulky frame away from the railing. He puffed out
his chest. "I ain't no boy."

Cezarne canted her head, letting her eyes roam freely over his muscular torso and stubbled jaw. She was well aware he was no boy. No, Dartanian Foxworthy was *all* man. It was a pity she had to keep him tied up.

"I'm well aware." She let her eyes take one last stroll along his chiselled form before nodding across the ocean. "You've done well to show me this, but I need the others if I'm to find the Lost City of Atlantis."

He quirked a brow, widening his stance against the rocking of the ship. "The Lost City? But no one has come close to finding it."

Trailing a finger along Dartanian's jaw, Cezarne clicked her tongue. "That's why they call it The *Lost* City." She palmed his cheek. "And you're going to lead me there."

"But I don't know where it is!"

"Ah, but that's where you're wrong, Mr. Foxworthy. I happen to know you were aboard the ship Bermuda before she went down." She knew this because she too was meant to be aboard. In fact, she was meant to captain the ship, only to be thwarted by the man before her. She let her hand slide from his face to his chest, pressing herself against him. "And I know what her destination was."

His eyes widened as he stumbled back, an incredulous laugh falling from his lips. "You're mad, you are. She never made it to her destination, did she? So how the bleedin' heck would I know where it is?"

Cezarne pointed her finger into his chest. "Because, as the lone survivor, you know where she went down. And you're going to take me there."

He reared back as if she'd slapped him, his gaze seeking out Bilkins. "She's lost her damn mind, mate."

Without a blink of the eye, Bilkins was in front of Dartanian, his blade pressed to the soft flesh of his throat. "That's our captain you're talking about. You best show some respect."

Dartanian swallowed thickly and nodded. "Yes, sir."

Bilkins held the knife firm, allowing a trickle of blood to lazily drip down Dartanian's neck before he stepped back. He wiped the blade on a kerchief and shoved it back into its scabbard.

"Now that that's settled." Cezarne took her place behind the wheel, spinning it counterclockwise. The ship sliced through the water towards the islands. "Where do we go from here?"

Dartanian hesitated briefly before stumbling back to the bow. His head swivelled this way and that, his lips moving in silent conversation with himself. "That way." He raised his bound hands and pointed northwest, around the island cluster and rock face.

"Very well then." She adjusted the wheel.

"No, I meant *around* the islands." Dartanian turned to her with a frown. "You're headed right for them."

She smiled. "Exactly."

Closing his eyes, he made the sign of the cross with his hands.

"Have a little faith, Mr. Foxworthy." She cackled, turning her attention to the crow's nest above. "What see you, Bones?"

A scraggly haired man poked his head over the side. "Just them there rocks and islands, Cap'n." He pointed a long finger. "Naught else but sea."

Cezarne nodded. "Keep watching. We'll lose light soon, and I don't want any surprises."

"Aye, aye, Cap'n." He cleared his throat before hollering, "And them rocks, Cap'n?"

"What of them?"

"Beggin' your pardon, Cap'n, but we're lookin' ta hit 'em."

Cezarne pulled her looking glass from her pocket and raised it to her eye. "So we are." She smirked, holding her hands firm on the wheel. If this was going to work, she needed to keep true.

The sun had all but disappeared now, and in its place was a sliver of a moon. Barely a glint of light was cast across the ocean waves, allowing them to see very little. Cezarne drew on her other senses. The feel of The Rose beneath her feet, the smell of salty air whipping her hair, the sound of waves crashing in the distance. The rocks were fast approaching.

"Cap'n?" Bones called once more, his voice unsteady.

"Not yet." Cezarne braced herself. Stories told of tumultuous waves surrounding the triangle, and this cluster of islands being the first point, she was expecting the worst. Many a captain had tried but failed to sail across the triangle, present company included, but Cezarne was not about to be another statistic.

The Rose creaked as the waves grew in size and ferocity. Cezarne shifted her feet, her eyes zeroed in on the blackness in front of them. Dartanian had lowered himself to the deck, his head on his knees as he mumbled prayers to whatever God would listen.

"Cap'n?" Bones cried out, worry and confusion colouring his tone.

Bilkins rushed to the bow, leaning as far over the rails as possible. "Almost!" He held his hand out behind him, palm down, as he watched. "Almost!"

Cezarne waited with bated breath for the signal.

"Now!" Bilkins called as he flipped his hand up.

Cezarne spun the wheel hard right, and the ship groaned as it fought the waves. There was a grinding from below as the keel connected with land, but not enough to bring them to a halt. The Rose narrowly missed the jutting rocks as she turned eastward.

At the helm, Cezarne watched the rocks until they were at their backs before spinning the wheel back the other way. The first hurdle was complete.

Bilkins bellowed, pumping a fist in the air. "We made it!"

Cezarne couldn't help but smile, though she knew they still had a way to go. For the past five years, Cezarne had pored over maps and coordinates, marking out each sunken ship and their trajectories.

Everything pointed to this one area, and now that she had confirmation of the Bermuda's whereabouts, she knew she was on the right track.

Now, past the point of no return, The Rose sailed on smooth seas beneath an eerily quiet sky. Even the ship herself had ceased her creaks and moans as she rocked Dartanian to sleep in her arms. Bilkins and Bones had taken their leave, getting what rest they could before the true test ahead of them. The veil.

As dawn broke several hours later, The Rose picked up speed, gliding through the cresting waves with ease. In the crow's nest, Bones held his looking glass aloft, scanning their surrounds. "There!" he called down the mast, his eyes bright with excitement.

Cezarne followed his pointing finger, bringing her own looking glass to her eye. A slow smile curled her lips. "You beautiful man, Bones! You've found it!" She adjusted the wheel, correcting their course.

Dartanian stared across the ocean, a frown marring his face. "*That* is The Lost City?" He shook his head. "You're even crazier than I thought if you think two stone pillars is a city." He shot a furtive glance towards Bilkins.

"Ye of little faith." Cezarne smirked. Of course the stone pillars weren't The Lost City. They were just the doorway. "Bilkins, hoist the mainsail."

"Aye, aye, Captain."

A flurry of wind caught the sail and The Rose lurched forward, her hull creating waves of her own.

The carved mermaid on the bowsprit pointed towards their target; the centre of the two pillars.

"What are you… You can't be meaning to go between them?" Dartanian marched towards her with an air of rebellion. "You're mad. She'll never make it."

"I am, and she will." Cezarne narrowed her eyes on the man before her. She'd never known him to be a coward. "You're quite welcome to go below deck if you're scared, Mr. Foxworthy. Hell, you can jump overboard if you're that worried. I have no use of you now." She waved him away, knowing full well he'd never jump. Dartanian Foxworthy was the only captain of the seven seas she knew to be averse to swimming.

"Ah, Cap'n?" Bones hung his head over the side, peering down at her. "Me eyes are fixin' ta show me somethin' funny." He glanced ahead then back to her. "Is the air… Is it a wobblin'?"

"Never to mind, Bones. All is well." She grinned, surging full steam ahead.

"Would you look at that?" Bilkins came to stand beside her, a mischievous glint in his eyes. "You were bloody right, Captain." He slapped a hand to her shoulder before hooting out a laugh. "Right where you said an' all."

Sweeping her hand out to her side, Cezarne took a bow. "Of course I was, Bilkins. Did you ever doubt me?"

"Not a once." He stared out at the shimmering air hanging between the pillars. "Not a once."

"What is that?" Dartanian asked, his mouth agape. He stumbled to the bow, hanging onto the railing as he squinted his eyes. "A mirage?"

"It's the veil."

"The veil?"

"*Through the veil of the sea...*"

"—the city of Atlantis waits for me," he finished for her, his eyes wide.

"Precisely."

The stone pillars with crumbling edges loomed ever closer, the gap between them seeming to narrow farther. *This is it,* she thought, bracing herself for impact.

Dartanian dropped to his knees, his hands still holding firm to the railings as he peered through the gaps. Bilkins stood beside him, facing the veil head on. Above, Bones had swung his legs over the crow's nest and shimmied down the mizzenmast to land beside Cezarne with a thud.

"Hold on!" she cried, wrenching the wheel side-to-side.

The Rose smashed against one then the other pillar, and the air filled with the sound of splintering wood as the ship began to take on water.

"She's not gonna make it!" Bones cried, and for a brief moment, Cezarne wondered if she'd made a mistake. But then the glittering veil before them wrapped itself around The Rose like a cloak, enveloping them in its embrace. The pillars disappeared, and the sky turned a deep purple, then black, as if night had fallen early.

Silence, but for the shuffling of Dartanian's feet. "Are we dead?" he asked.

"Of course not," Bilkins said gruffly. "Right?"

"I don't think so." Cezarne walked in a circle around the wheel. She could hear nothing. No water rushing in, no waves crashing. Nothing. Perhaps they *had* died, for as far as she was aware, ships could not mend themselves.

Unsure of their fate or even how to navigate without the stars to guide her, Cezarne let The Rose lead the way. After a few minutes, a tiny beacon of light took shape, growing until they could see lush green lands.

Blinking away the dark, Cezarne took in her surroundings. It was like nothing she'd ever seen before, and yet familiar all at the same time. Stone pillars with deep green vines clinging to them stuck up from the ground, and large leafy trees hung across the river they now appeared to be gliding down. The iridescent sky above was coloured in shades of pink, blue, and green.

The Rose followed the river around a curve where trees laden with golden fruit lined the edges, and beyond them, a large stone statue of a man dressed in robes towered.

"I don't believe it," Dartanian said in awe. "We're really here." He pointed at the statue. "I've seen his likeness before."

"His name is Atlas, son of Poseidon, and he was the ruler of these lands." Cezarne turned to Bones. "Lower the anchor. I should like to look around."

While he scurried off, she continued. "Some say he built a temple of gold in honour of his father. One so large it's said to reach the clouds above." She tilted her head back, taking in the beatific colours streaking the sky. "A tribute fitting for the creator of this oasis."

The clanking of the anchor ruptured the silence, giving them pause. Birds took flight, darting across the river and up into the skies. The Rose lurched to a stop, and Bilkins pushed the gangplank out to rest along the shore. With Cezarne in the lead, they each walked across the plank and to the land.

"This way," she said, traipsing through thick foliage towards the statue. If her readings had been correct, what she sought would be at his feet.

"How do you know where you're going?" Dartanian asked as he swiped branches away from his face with a huff. "Anyone would think you'd been here before."

"Ah." Cezarne touched her finger to the side of her nose. "That would be telling now, wouldn't it, Mr. Foxworthy?"

He turned to Bones with a thumb hooked in Cezarne's direction. "Does she always talk in riddles like this?"

"Aye, she does." He sniggered. "Tis what ya like 'bout her."

Dodging a swinging vine, Dartanian scoffed. "I don't think so."

Bones guffawed, shaking his head. "Righto then." He marched ahead, using his cutlass to carve a path.

"There he is," Bilkins said in reverence as he stared up at the behemoth statue. "The mighty Atlas."

"A fine specimen if ever I saw one." Cezarne winked, barrelling ahead to the plinth he rested on. She climbed atop a ridge running around the bottom edge and peered between the statue's legs. "A sight to behold." She turned to Bilkins with a grin. "It's here."

"Bring him," Bilkins called back to Bones, who in turn nudged Dartanian forward.

"A right treat an' all, init?" He gestured for Dartanian to join their captain on the plinth. With a confused look over his shoulder, he obliged. Cezarne had her hands in a large bowl of water resting between Atlas's feet.

"What's all this then?"

Cezarne held her cupped hands out to him. "Drink."

Dartanian scrunched his nose. "I don't think so."

Her brows lowered, and she scowled at him. "Drink," she said again, forcefully.

Huffing out a sigh, Dartanian leaned his head forward, wrapping his lips around the tips of her fingers, and suckled the water until it was gone. Cezarne's eyes searched his, waiting.

"How do you feel?"

He blinked once, twice, three times. "I feel…" His eyes darted about, as if seeing their surrounds for the first time. "Where are we?" His voice was quiet, filled with awe, until he looked down to see his hands were tied. Raising them to her, he asked, "Why are my hands bound? What's going on?"

Cezarne grinned, reaching her hand to palm his cheek. "We found it," she whispered, glancing up at the statue.

Dartanian followed her gaze, stumbling back and falling to the ground. "Is that…?" Cezarne nodded. "And this is…?"

She nodded again. "Atlantis."

His eyes widened, his mouth opening and closing. "We found it," he whispered. Then, shaking his head, he frowned. "But, how? The last thing I remember was the Bermuda." He winced, his cheeks flaming. "Sorry about that, by the way."

Cezarne shook her head dismissively. "Water under the bridge. Continue."

He turned his gaze skyward. "The Bermuda was hit by a storm out of nowhere, and she went down. And then…" He shook his head.

"Go on."

"You'll think me foolish."

"Try me."

He closed his eyes, sucking in a breath. "I remember seeing a… a mermaid, or at least something that looked like a mermaid, with long flowing hair and a tail. She carried me to safety."

Cezarne nodded. When he'd been found washed ashore with no recollection of who he was, she'd had her suspicions. Lore spoke of mermaids granting safety to those found in the sea but, as with all mystical creatures, their help does not come for free. The price; your memories.

"What you speak is true, my love. That's why I had to find the elixir of Atlas." She smiled, caressing his cheek. "I couldn't have you forgetting me."

He grasped her hand. "I could never forget you."

Bones snorted. "Told ya. Them riddles is what ya like." He clapped his hand to Dartanian's shoulder. "Good ta 'ave ya back, sir."

"Bones, Bilkins." Dartanian pushed up from the ground, only now noticing his fellow shipmates. He held his hands, still bound, out to them both. Bones took hold, shaking them both, but Bilkins turned his nose up, huffing sullenly.

"You're still sore about the Bermuda, I take it, Bilkins? I *am* sorry."

"And well you should be too. We're a team, we are. You deserted us." He pointed a finger at Dartanian's chest. "And you hurt the captain." He jutted his chin, and Dartanian nodded his agreement.

"That I did, and I promise to make up for it however she sees fit." He turned his attention back to the blonde-haired beauty. "Can you ever forgive me?"

Tapping a finger to her chin, she walked in a slow circle. "Hmmm, let me think. I suppose you *did* help me find what I've spent my life looking for." She grinned, wrapping her arms around his neck and planting a kiss upon his lips. "It's only fair."

Atlantis *was an entry for the* Sunday Star Times *short story competition. There was no theme to follow, only a 3000-word limit. I wrote 2999!*

**A little fun fact for you**
*When I was a teenager, I worked at the local library, and there was a member there with the name Cezarne. I'd never seen any name more beautiful before, and it stuck with me. It seemed only fitting to be the name of my buccaneering captain.*

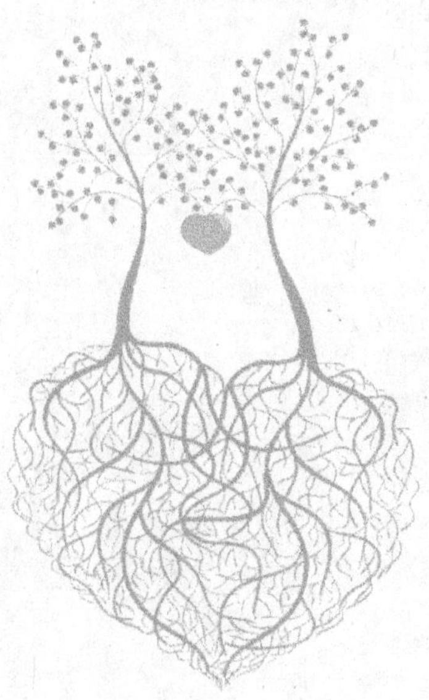

# Love, Pure and Simple

Stories and poems about love, reciprocated and unrequited.

# The Secret

"PINKIE PROMISE?" I hold my hand out, my little finger extended.

"Pinkie promise." Sarah wraps her finger around mine in an embrace.

"Cross your heart and hope to die?" I raise my brow in a smirk. It seems so childish, but it's the way we've always done it.

"Stick a needle in my eye." She grins before running her finger and thumb across her lips. "Your secret is safe with me."

Butterflies dance in my stomach. This is it. I'm about to let my best friend in on something I've kept to myself for so long. Too long. I feel almost giddy with relief, like the secret is bubbling up from inside, ready to burst free.

"Okay." I lean in close, whispering the words in her ear.

Her eyes widen, and her mouth drops open. I pull back, my teeth finding the corner of my lip. *What will she say? What will she think?*

So many emotions play out across her face, and I feel as though I might cry.

*Say something. Anything.*

My eyes drop to my hands in my lap. A stray thread holds my attention as my world slowly crumbles around me.

*I will not cry. Not now.*

After what feels like an eternity, her delicate hand slips into my line of sight. She reaches for my hand, lacing her fingers with mine. I chance a peek at her face, and what I see takes my breath away.

*She understands.*

"I feel the same way," she whispers with a smile.

*The bond between friends is sometimes stronger than we think, and I love the idea of two friends falling for each other and one taking that first scary step of admitting it.*

# You Promised Me

You promised me a kiss,
But gave me so much more.
You took my breath away,
And had me sinking to the floor.

You promised me your love,
Unwavering and true.
You gave my life a purpose,
And that was loving you.

You promised me forever,
'til death unto us part.
You said the words I needed.
You spoke right to my heart.

You promised me an always,
Together we'd grow old.
But here I am without you,
You're not doing what you told.

You promised me eternal,
We'd live forevermore.
But Death had other plans,
He was calling at your door.

You promised me, my dear,
That our love would see us through.
But you promised the impossible,
And now I'm missing you.

*This is probably my favourite poem (that I've written).*

*I drew inspiration from a number of things. The beginning is drawn from my own relationship with my husband, and the end was inspired by a friend who recently lost hers.*

# Queen of my Heart

BRIGHT, CHERRY RED. The colour that would be the end of our relationship.

Clark had said goodbye with a chaste kiss to my cheek, reminding me of his after-work function that would end late. He told me not to wait up.

I didn't.

As soon as six-thirty rolled around, I dug out my fishnet stockings from the back of my drawer and pulled them on with a slinky white dress. My make-up was simple; mascara, eyeshadow and a swipe of champagne lippy. My hair was piled on my head with curls falling around my face in a delicate frame. I was a knockout.

The club was busier than I remembered. A chorus of *It's Raining Men* played on the speakers while a group of queens wiggled their asses on stage. I sidled up to the bar and ordered a Jim and coke, hold the ice. Jimmy smiled, waving my money away. "It's on the house."

With a wink, I swirled my straw around my glass before taking a sip and turning my back, leaning against the bar.

"It's been a while," he said.

"Too long," I muttered under my breath.

The worries of the day slowly faded as I let the music seep into my soul. I needed this.

Applause filled the room, drawing my attention to the stage. The unmistakable first line of Gloria Gaynor's *I Will Survive* pumped out of the speakers and everyone around me jumped to their feet, whooping and hollering. One slim leg poked through the curtain followed by a glittery emerald-green torso. Cherry-red lips and a wave of auburn hair danced across the stage, holding the audience captive. Plump, cherry-red lips and eyes that reminded me of Clark. I couldn't look away. It was wrong to be thinking of another man while he was out schmoosing clients and earning us money, but I'm only human, and it had been so long since he'd looked at me with desire.

Sculling back my drink, I pushed Clark from my mind and wound my way through the crowd and up onto the stage. He didn't bat an eye as I shimmied my way closer, my hands roaming up his chest to rest on his shoulders. I swayed alongside him, matching every twist of his hips with ease.

Those cherry lips held me captive as they wrapped around the mic to belt out the final notes of the song. I couldn't help myself. I leaned in and pressed my lips to his. When I pulled back, his eyes danced with amusement. "How did you know?" he asked in surprise.

My brow creased in confusion. "Know what?" I searched his eyes, seeing disappointment as he shook his head. Realisation dawned on me. "Clark?" I whispered.

*As soon as I heard the prompt, cherry-red lipstick, I immediately pictured drag queens all dolled up in their heavy make-up and sequined dresses. I thought it was a nice play to have them both be drag queens, only one gave it up for their relationship, while the other secretly started.*

# My Everything

There was something about him
I couldn't ignore.
Something so special
I had to adore.

There was something about him
That spoke to my soul.
Something so tortured
Yet beautifully whole.

There was something about him
That awoke my desire.
Something so sensual
It filled me with fire.

There was something about him
I needed to hold.
Something so flawless,
Amazing and bold.

There was something about him;
This man oh so fine.
Something about him
I had to make mine.

*Often when I'm struggling to come up with something to fit the assignment, I'll fall to poetry – something I've really only started writing since joining the group. Back when I was a teenager, I'd written the odd prose, but it wasn't until recently that I really started getting into it.*

*My inspiration for this piece was my husband. I thought back to when we first met and how I felt. We actually met at work; a factory where we built ovens. We were on separate lines, but I remember noticing how beautiful his eyes were. Not only that, he always smelled delicious. After a bit of back and forth flirting, I decided to bite the bullet and make him mine! The rest, as they say, is history!*

# Unrequited

Your eyes they are so blue
So deep I could just drown.
Your hair dark like the night sky,
Though others might say brown.

Your smile could light up any room,
Filled with so much charm.
Oh how I wish it was I
Who could be on your arm.

You make me laugh, you make me smile,
You bring a tear to my eye.
For to you I am but no one,
Just a person passing by.

You know not that I'm here
Awaiting your attention.
For even but a moment
Of your love and your affection.

So I shall sit and wait,
Admiring from afar.
Until the day you notice
I'm forever where you are.

*From one extreme to another. Unrequited was an assignment to write a poem about unrequited love. This one actually came to me as I was out for a walk, and it suddenly hit me.*
*I think it's one of my favourite poems I've written.*

# Love Always

WITH A FLICK OF HIS WRIST, Greg unfurled the tablecloth and smoothed it down. He set out two placemats and their finest cutlery. A bottle of wine sat in an ice bucket to the side, with two glasses gleaming in the candlelight, and in the centre of the table, he placed a vase with a single red rose. Her favourite. He stood back and surveyed his work, checking it was everything it should be. Everything she'd want.

February 14th had rolled around much faster than he was expecting. The one day of the year to cause him so much angst. It seemed like only yesterday he had been arguing with his wife Karen about yet another failed Valentine's Day on his behalf. What did she expect though? He had never been the most romantic of men, and he'd never kept it a secret. Even on their first date he'd shown up empty-handed, with a shrug and a smile, saying "No frills with me, babe, sorry." At first, she had found it endearing, but over the years it had become a bone of contention between them.

You see, Karen was a heart-on-her-sleeve romantic. She believed in showering everyone with love and affection all through the year, but especially on Valentine's Day. In her eyes, it was a day to be celebrated and cherished, and she always went to such pains to make it memorable.

Every year, it was the same. She'd gleefully hand over the gift she'd spent hours searching for and wrapping with care, only to be met with a chuckle and a "You know I don't remember this stuff, babe." Each time he'd watch her heart break a little more, and each time he'd die a little inside for causing that sparkle in her eyes to dim.

It's not that he wanted to be an arse, he just never saw the need to buy into it all. Why only show your loved ones you love them on that one day? Didn't he show her enough by marrying her and providing a comfortable life? Didn't he show her by choosing her to be by his side each and every day of his life? Why did he have to make a big song and dance about it all? It just wasn't his style.

Of course, she never expected him to shower her with jewellery or expensive gifts. He knew she'd have been happy with a simple flower from the garden or a love note left on the kitchen bench. But he couldn't even muster that small effort once a year to show her he was thinking of her. Instead, he'd huff about the conglomerate corporations making bank on a day they'd deemed the day of love. He didn't need to buy her gifts or tell her how he felt just because they told him to. She *knew* he loved her. Didn't she?

He shook his head. She had to have known. She couldn't have gone without knowing how he truly felt about her.

The unwanted flashbacks bounced around in his head, a constant reminder of the day that would be forever seared into his brain. The day he wished to God he could go back and do-over.

February 14th, 2020. It had started like every Valentine's Day; with Karen rolling over and planting a kiss on his cheek. "Happy Valentine's Day, my love." And then she'd pulled a parcel out from behind her back. "Open it," she'd said with a grin.

It was a first edition copy of his favourite childhood book, *Peter Rabbit.* "Wow, that must've cost a pretty penny," he'd said, flicking through the pages.

"You're worth every penny, my love."

He'd placed it on the nightstand, a gruff "thanks" said as he sat up. He didn't miss the look in her eyes as he swung his legs around to get up. "Sorry, babe. I didn't get you anything. You know how it is. I'd forget my birthday if you weren't here to remind me." He'd laughed, avoiding her eyes while he tied his robe.

She'd rolled onto her back, her hands clasped across her belly as she stared at the ceiling.

"I'll try and remember next year, eh? Maybe I'll surprise you one of these days."

She didn't say a word. Not a single thing as she'd dragged herself out of bed. He'd watched as she donned her yoga pants and runners. He'd stood by as she pulled her hair up into a messy bun before grabbing her phone and earbuds. And even though he knew she was upset, she'd still placed a hand to his chest, going up on tiptoes to press a kiss to his lips. "Happy Valentine's Day," she'd whispered as she stepped out the door for the last time.

When the cops had knocked on his door an hour later, he'd dropped to his knees, a keening noise forcing its way out through the lips she'd kissed only that morning. They'd told him a car had taken the corner too fast, right at the same time she was crossing the road. It had been quick, they'd said. She wouldn't have felt any pain. But he knew. He knew that though she might not have felt pain from the impact of the car breaking every bone of her body, she was still in pain. Pain that he had caused because he couldn't take the time to show her on that one day that meant so much to her, that he loved her too.

He placed her urn in the spot opposite him, along with the silver frame they'd been given as a wedding gift. Her beautiful smiling face shining out at him from beneath her veil as she stood proudly by his side on what was the happiest day of his life. Yet another thing he'd neglected to let her in on. His hands gripped the back of the chair as he stared at the photo before he took a deep breath and sat down, wishing he could hold her hand once more. "I'm sorry I never made the effort when you were here to appreciate it, babe, but this one's for you." His eyes welled up as he held his wine glass in the air. "I love you, babe. Always have and always will."

Love Always *was a writing prompt from the site Reedsy:* Start your story with one character setting up a romantic dinner, and end it with them looking at a framed wedding photo.
*They post writing prompts every week. You can check out further prompts and stories from their site* https://blog.reedsy.com/creative-writing-prompts/

# Two Hearts

Broken-hearted
Walking solo
Envy in my eyes.
Couple strolling
Hand in hand
But I am only I.

Sad and lonely
Contemplating
Where did I go wrong?
Hands in pockets
Scuffing toes
Ambling along.

Eyes averted
Staring solemnly
At the ground below.
Too disheartened
Didn't notice
Another lonely soul.

Shoulders bustle
Hands go up
Ready to placate.
Eyes collide
Time stands still
Could this be fate?

Slow smile
Recognition
Heart is beating fast.
Reaching out
Taking hold
This stranger from my past.

Two hearts
Find each other
On this fateful day.
Two hands
Bind together
Forever will they stay.

Two Hearts *was written first thing one morning after
I'd been asked to submit a poem for an anthology
with the theme of Serendipity. I had only ten days to
come up with something, and this one kind of came to
me upon waking. Slightly different rhythm to what I
would normally write, so I quite enjoyed it.*

# The Suitor

"GIANCARLO, YOU'VE GOT TO HELP ME!" Raoul cried as he threw himself dramatically across the counter. "Lucious is holding a dance to find a suitor, and I have nothing to wear!"

Giancarlo pursed his lips and quirked a brow. "How long have you been working for me?"

"Two years."

"Exactly. Two years, and you're leaving it until the last minute? You should know better." He waggled a finger through the air, tutting. "Don't you know it takes time to look this good?" He gestured towards his charcoal-grey suit with fine pinstripes of red woven into the fabric. "It doesn't just come off the rack like this, darling."

"But you can help me, right?"

Giancarlo skirted around the counter, taking Raoul's hands in his. "Of course I can help you. They don't call me the fairy godmother of fashion for nothing, you know." He winked, dropping Raoul's hand and spinning on his heel. "Follow me." Sashaying to the end of the room, he pulled open a curtain with a flourish, and Raoul gasped. With a look over his shoulder, Giancarlo simply said, "I know, right? This is my private collection, reserved only for very important occasions, such as this." Giancarlo trailed his fingers lovingly over the fabrics as he sauntered down the racks, his lips pursed to one side in concentration. "Ah, yes, here it is." He pulled out a deep mahogany double-breasted jacket with a black and white pocket square, matching mahogany slacks, and a crisp white shirt. "This is the one."

"It's beautiful."

"Of course it is, darling. Chris Hemsworth ordered it for the Oscars tomorrow night," Giancarlo scoffed, handing the suit over with care. "This needs to be back here in pristine condition, no later than midnight, or Chris will have my arse, and not in a good way." He waggled his brows suggestively, and Raoul chuckled as he hurriedly undressed, kicking his scuffed shoes to the side. Giancarlo eyed them and tutted. "No, these will not do." Marching to the back wall, he found a pair of tan leather shoes with buckles on the side. "These." He sat them on the floor away from the tattered ones, as if being in the same vicinity could tarnish them. As Raoul pulled on the jacket, Giancarlo fussed about, smoothing imaginary creases and making clucking noises in the back of his throat. "You're a little slimmer in the waist and not so broad in the chest, but it's the best I can do on such short notice." Flicking his wrist in the air, he checked the time and gasped. "You have ten minutes to get there. Make every second count." He ushered Raoul out the door with a final pat down. "And remember, midnight and pristine condition!"

The dance was in full swing when Raoul arrived. Stopping outside the doors, he inhaled deeply to settle his nerves before adjusting his jacket for the millionth time. "You've got this," he whispered to himself as he pushed the doors open and made a beeline for the dancefloor.

Lucious wasn't hard to spot in his royal-blue waistcoat with the sleeves of his shirt rolled up to his elbows. His golden hair flicked about as he danced to the music pumping through the speakers, and his eyes gleamed with an ever-present joy. All around him women dressed to the nines shimmied and shook, gyrating towards him in an attempt to seek his favour.

"It's now or never." Raoul walked straight up to him, holding his hand out in question. "May I have this dance?"

Lucious stopped and stared at his proffered hand. "Raoul? What are you doing here?"

Raoul swallowed the lump in his throat, willing the butterflies in his stomach to stand still. "I… I came for you."

"You…" Lucious shook his head, running a hand through his golden locks. "You're here for me?"

"Who else would I be here for?" He waved a hand at the dancing women who were now watching with interest. "Certainly not any of them."

A slow smile graced Lucious's lips. "They're not really my type either. It was father's idea." He stepped forward, taking the hand still waiting for him. "I'd love to dance with you."

Their hands entwined, they swayed together until the clock began to strike twelve, and Raoul reluctantly pulled away. "I'm sorry, but I have to go before I turn into a pumpkin. This face needs at least seven hours of beauty sleep." He fluttered his lashes, framing his face with his hands before darting towards the door.

"Wait! When can I see you again?"

"Anytime you like. I'm sure you know where to find me." He winked, dropping Giancarlo's business card on the floor behind him.

The Suitor *was a fun assignment where we had to do a fairy tale retelling, and* Cinderella *was the first one to pop into my head. I instantly knew I wanted it to be about a man and his fashion designer fairy godmother.*
*This has since been written into a full length novel of the same name (under my pen name, Cyan Tayse).*

# A Moment in Time

Sticky sap oozes over hard, knotted wood
Leaves gently whisper on the breeze.
Birds sing a chorus from high up yonder
As they build their nests with ease.

Down below, in the shade, I rest my weary head
Staring up at the dappled sky of blue
All around the world continues turning,
But I am stuck on thoughts of you.

The way your laugh would make me smile,
The twinkle in your eyes so bright.
The way your arms could bring such comfort
On a cold and lonely night.

You were my rock, my saving grace,
My anchor in choppy ocean waves.
You guided me and kept me sane,
Even through some close shaves.

Beneath our tree, I sit and wonder
As tears slide down my cheek,
If I could've changed our ending,
If only I weren't so weak.

A single breath, a moment in time
Was all it took to lose
The one who meant the world to me,
The one I'd always choose.

In the shade of our tree, with closed eyes, I lay,
No more dappled sky of blue do I see,
No more songs from birds up high,
Just thoughts of you and me.

*This one came out of nowhere. I was going through my assignments and instant writing exercises and came across one where we had to describe being a character up in a tree, and for some reason, that stood out to me. I took the parts I liked most and wrote them into the first paragraph of this poem, and then the rest kind of flowed from there.*

# Respect

"SO, WHAT DO YOU THINK?" Joe leans back in his seat, his legs spread wide and one arm dangling between them.

"What do I think?" I stare at him, not quite sure how to form a coherent sentence to respond.

"Yeah. I mean, like I said…" He sits forward, swiping his thumb across his nose. "It's going to benefit both of us. You especially." The crooked grin he gives me would've melted my insides once upon a time. Now all it does is make me want to punch him in his stupid face.

I run my tongue along my front teeth, closing my eyes and inhaling deeply to keep myself from acting on my impulses. What he's suggesting is the most arrogant, misogynistic idea I've ever heard, and he's staring at me as if he's a genius doing me a huge favour. And sure, to his mates, he probably would seem that way if I were to go along with this cockamamie bullshit, but thanks to my Aretha Franklin phase in my adolescence, I have more self-respect than that.

"As tempting as the offer is, I'm gonna have to say no."

He frowns, taking hold of my hands. "Babe, come on. Think about it. You get all of this—" he runs a hand down his torso as if he's some sort of delectable treat, "—with none of the pressure to perform for me in the bedroom every night."

"Oh gee, when you put it that way…"

His lips curl into a slow grin. "I knew you'd agree."

"…It's still a hard no from me." Dragging my hand out of his grasp, I stand, hooking my bag over my shoulder. "I'll grab my things in the morning." With my head held high, I march for the door without so much as a second glance. Even his big brown puppy-dog eyes won't stop me from walking out.

"Babe," he calls, but I ignore him, waving my hand over my shoulder. I'm not his babe anymore, and if I'm honest, I haven't been for months. What could have been a beautiful relationship changed swiftly the second I moved into his cramped one-bedroom apartment. All of a sudden I went from being the sexy girlfriend to the live-in surrogate mother, taking care of all the cooking and cleaning while also holding down a full time job. He'd come home and sprawl on the couch, gaming or scrolling through his phone, oblivious to me cleaning around him, and never lifting his finger unless it was to push a button on the remote.

And he has the audacity to suggest an open relationship where he gets his end away elsewhere, while I sit at home waiting for him like a good little girlfriend, and say it's for *my* benefit. I don't think so.

I should've run for the hills the moment I saw his overflowing sink and laundry hamper, but like a lovesick puppy, I ignored the signs. It's funny what a few months can do for your perspective.

From now on, I'm flying solo. I'm going my own way. I'm—

"Oof." My face explodes in pain, my phone clatters to the floor, as does my bag, and I stumble backwards. Two firm hands grab hold of my arms, catching me before I lose my balance completely.

"Shit, are you okay?" Four of the brightest blue eyes stare back at me, and all thoughts of being a strong, independent woman fly out the window never to be seen again.

I blink up at him, my nose and forehead throbbing.

He waves his hand in front of my face. "How many fingers am I holding up?"

"Uh, three?" I manage, though I don't sound convincing to my own ears. Bright spots dance before my eyes, but I'm almost positive of my answer.

"Phew. You had me worried there. I know I can be a Neanderthal, but I didn't think my head was that dense to give you a concussion." He rubs his hand against the back of his head.

It takes me a minute to connect the dots between my throbbing face and his Neanderthal head, but when it finally clicks, I'm sure my face turns a lovely shade of crimson. "Oh my... shit, are *you* okay?" I reach for his shoulders, spinning him around so I can examine the back of his head.

He chuckles, and the sound vibrates through my hands. "I'm fine. Should've been looking where I was going."

"I ran into you. I think it's me who should've been paying attention. I'm so sorry."

"Honestly, I'm fine." He stoops down, picking up my phone and handing it to me. His lips pull into a thin line as he tentatively runs a finger along my forehead, eliciting a hiss from me. "Are you sure *you're* okay? That's quite the bump."

"To be honest, I'm more embarrassed than hurt. I can't believe I ran into you like that. I'm such a klutz." A klutz with a pounding head.

He shrugs. "Accidents happen. And you obviously had a lot on your mind." He glances behind me. "You're up in 5A, right? With Joe?"

"I was, yeah." I offer him a sheepish smile. "You could say I just handed in my notice."

His eyebrows lift, and he tucks his hands in his pockets. "That's unfortunate for Joe."

I roll my eyes, then wince at the sharp jolt of pain that follows. "Believe me, he won't be pining over me. In fact, I'd be surprised if he doesn't have someone in the wings already waiting after the conversation we just had."

He sucks a breath in through his teeth. "Sounds like you're better off without him."

I pull myself up taller, nodding. "I am. I can't be what he needs me to be, and he's definitely not what I need or want."

"Well, uh…" He chuckles. "Sorry, I don't even know your name."

"Candace."

"Well, Candace, it's his loss. For what it's worth, I think he's an idiot."

A laugh bubbles up and out. "You don't even know me."

"I like to think of myself as a pretty good judge of character, and you, Candace, seem like a genuinely nice person. One I wouldn't mind getting to know better. It's a pity we met under such circumstances." He offers a smile and holds out his hand. "I'm Mark, by the way."

His hand is warm, his shake firm, solid, and when he smiles, his eyes light up. "Mark." The word rolls off my tongue like a caress, and I gently slide my hand from his. "Maybe I'll see you around sometime." Grabbing my bag from the floor, I give him a nod as I step around him. "It was nice bumping into you."

*This one was inspired by conversations with friends, and the song "Flowers" by Miley Cyrus. So many times we read stories of women who are pushovers or too shy for their own good, and I wanted to have a strong character who knows her worth.*

# Yearbook

BALLBREAKER. That's what they called her, because she was good at taking the prosecution by the balls and bringing them to their knees. Kate spent her days defending criminals and getting them off Scott free. She didn't like to say it was her calling, but it took a certain type of person to be able to put their morals aside and do such a thing, and Kate excelled at it. She prided herself in being the smartest in the room. Always. She had to be at the top of her game every single day. She had to show them she wasn't a pushover, and she wasn't one to play games. Cross her, and you'd know about it.

But today… today was a day she wished she wasn't so good at her job. Today was a day she'd regret forever.

Pulling into the garage, she let the car idle while she stretched her neck side-to-side. The courthouse chairs are not known for their comfort, and she couldn't wait to get inside and let the overstuffed cushions of her couch envelop her. She switched the car off and grabbed her briefcase from the passenger seat. After unlocking the front door, she threw her keys into the bowl on the armoire, then double checked each of the deadbolts were pulled and locked. Kicking her shoes off, she padded through to her bedroom, unzipping her tapered skirt as she went. Her sweatpants were calling her, as was a large glass of pinot gris.

With some smooth jazz playing on the stereo, Kate grabbed her laptop and sat on the couch. She pushed the screen up and pressed the button to boot it up. While she waited, she poured herself a much-needed wine and sat back. It had been a rough day. One she was desperate to put behind her.

*We find the defendant, not guilty, Your Honour.*

She shook her head. She should be happy. It was the outcome she strived for. But this one stung more than most. Her mind conjured images of the blonde-haired teen with the haunted expression in her eyes, sitting obediently beside her lawyer at the front of the courtroom. The strength she showed to point out her attacker; the man sitting to Kate's right. The way she articulated every little detail of what happened to her, and then the way her face dropped when the verdict was read out.

*Not guilty.*

She'd done her job, and done it well, but at what cost? That sweet young girl would have to live with the ramifications of what Monroe Wilson did to her—because she knew in her heart that he did. She would be plagued with fear and anger, even hate towards men, and for what? So Monroe could get his jollies from overpowering someone half his size? It wasn't right.

*Not guilty, Your Honour.*

There had been such a cacophony from the stalls at the reading of the verdict, and though she wanted to join them in their outrage, she couldn't. Beside her, Monroe sat with a shit-eating grin on his face, his meaty arm lifting to wrap around her shoulders and pull her into his sweat-soaked armpit. It had taken everything in her not to shudder at his embrace. Not to break down and cry at the sight of that poor, sweet girl sitting with silent tears rolling down her cheeks.

Kate groaned, letting her head roll to the back of the couch. In all her years in defence, she'd never had a case hit her so hard. She scrubbed a hand down her face, then sat up just enough to take a sip of her wine.

Her laptop chimed as it came to life, and she leaned forward, staring at the blinking cursor requesting her password. With deft fingers, she hit the keys, and her home screen lit up. She ran her fingers across the mousepad, the cursor hovering over the case files she needed to read before tomorrow, but she couldn't face them. Not yet.

Instead, she pulled up Google. She'd overheard a group of baby lawyers talking about some new app where you could connect with people from all over the world. What had they called it? Class... no, Yearbook, that was it. Pulling her lip between her teeth, she took a breath and typed it into the search bar.

*Yearbook, the app to connect with friends, both old and new.*

Before she could overthink it, she clicked the link and signed up. Folding her legs beneath her, she took another swig of her wine then settled back into the couch. She filled in all the prompted details of her life; age, gender, school, occupation. She deliberated over which picture to upload as her profile, finally settling on a candid shot taken at a work luncheon a month earlier. It was one of few photos that caught her smiling.

Kate sat back, twisting her lips to the side as she clicked 'okay' and let Yearbook publish her profile. She went back to her homepage, and a list of 'suggested friends' popped up. Scrolling through, she considered each one carefully. There was the girl who rivalled her at every class, both striving for excellence. After clicking through her profile and seeing that she had indeed succeeded in becoming a surgeon, she selected the 'friend request' button.

There was the jock who'd tormented her through her dorky phase; before she'd had braces and her teeth still stuck out like Roger Rabbit. He was a definite no.

She was scrolling through a few others when a notification popped up. *Anaru Kahurangi requests your friendship.*

She paused. *Anaru Kahurangi.* Now that was a name she hadn't thought of in years. She followed the link to his page, and his green eyes and cheeky grin took her straight back to her sixteen-year-old self. He had been the new boy at school, and she had been tasked with showing him around. A normally confident girl, she'd floundered to find words when she looked into his eyes. His laugh would send warm tingles through her chest, and at times, her heart would beat so fast she'd thought it would burst.

He was the most beautiful specimen of man she'd ever seen, and aside from her being his tour guide, he didn't seem to know she existed. Long days had been spent daydreaming of Anaru wrapping her in his arms. Long nights too, if she was honest. She'd been in love with him, or at the very least, the idea of him. But that love was never reciprocated.

And now, all these years later, Anaru Kahurangi was reaching out to her.

She hesitated, unsure if she wanted to go down that road. Just seeing his smiling face brought all those feelings back to the surface, and she found herself longing to talk to him again.

*What could it hurt? It's just a simple click of the button.*

*And a one-way ticket to a broken heart.*

She chewed her lip, her finger poised over the mouse. *One little click.*

Closing her eyes, she sucked in a breath and pressed her finger down.

*You are now friends with Anaru Kahurangi.*

Moments later, a speech bubble popped up at the bottom of her screen. *Anaru Kahurangi wants to chat.*

Kate's heart thundered in her chest. She wasn't ready for that. She hadn't prepared; didn't know a thing about this older version of her high school crush. She hadn't expected him to contact her at all, let alone straight away.

Running her fingertip around the edge of her wine glass, she considered what to do. A little voice inside her mind told her to simply ignore it, but the louder part of her brain, the part that held social etiquette in high regard, wouldn't let her do that. Neither would her sixteen-year-old self who would've given anything to have him talk to her.

She leant forward, swiping the bottle off the table and pouring another healthy glug into her glass. A little Dutch courage would see her right. Pressing the speech bubble icon, she watched as a box appeared on her screen and three dots danced beside Anaru's picture. *Anaru is typing a message.*

**Hey, Kate. Long time no see.**

Without overthinking it, she quickly responded with, *Hey, Anaru. It's been a while for sure,* then sat back and waited.

**How are things? I see you're working in law like you always wanted. That's great.**

He knew about that? As far as she was aware, he barely even noticed her when she hadn't been showing him around campus. All this time she'd felt invisible, when apparently, he'd been paying more attention than she'd thought.

*Yeah, I am. Defence Attorney. It's not for everyone, but I'm good at it, and it pays the bills. How about you? What are you doing with yourself these days?*

She finished off her glass of wine and navigated back to his page. Scrolling through his pictures, she noted the lack of a Mrs. Kahurangi, and a tingle of promise settled in her stomach. It amazed her that all these years later his smile could still have that effect on her. She felt like a teenager all over again.

***Construction mainly. I've been helping my uncle out with his building firm. Ever since we went into lockdown, the housing market has gone nuts and everyone wants to build.***

Good with his hands? Check.

Kate chuckled to herself. She was being ridiculous. It was just a casual conversation with someone she used to know. That was all. Nothing more, nothing less. There was no point getting ahead of herself.

She placed her laptop on the coffee table and swung her feet onto the floor. She needed to play it cool.

*That's nice of you to help out. I'm sure he appreciates it. Fortunately for me, crime never stops, so there's always a need for lawyers.*

*True, true. Still, it must be difficult to do. I don't envy you.*

*You have to be good at compartmentalising. I have to put aside my beliefs and focus on the evidence. Some cases are harder than others.*

She sighed, closing her eyes. Monroe Wilson's smarmy face grinned out from the darkness. She'd wanted to get away from her work for a moment, not rehash it.

*But enough about me. Are you still playing rugby? Married? Father to a team of All Blacks?*

Smooth. Real smooth.

Three dots danced across the screen then stopped. They started up again, then stopped. Kate bit her lip. She'd ruined it already.

*Not married, and no children unfortunately. Never did find anyone who matched my… expectations. As for rugby, I play the odd social game now and then, but nothing competitive in years.*

*And you? Is there a Mr or Mrs on the scene?*

She couldn't help the way her heart jumped into her throat at his question. He was only being polite, responding in kind. It didn't mean he was fishing.

But a part of her wondered, no, hoped that perhaps she could be mistaken. What were these expectations of his? And why did he say it like that?

Instantly images of herself wrapped in his arms conjured in her mind, and though she knew it was silly, she let herself bask in it for a moment. A girl could dream after all.

*No. No Mr on the scene. I've never really found the time to date.*

She stared at her fingers as if they'd betrayed her. "What are you doing?" she hissed to herself. It was true, she hadn't had time to date with all the studying she needed to do to pass her bar exams, but that was years ago. She had no real excuse other than the fact that no one measured up to Anaru. No one made her feel the way he did, and that was saying something considering they'd barely spoken in the past.

It was ridiculous really. She was a fully grown woman now, and still she held onto her childhood crush, forever comparing how people made her feel to those intense emotions she'd felt in school. She'd watched him from afar, forever hoping he would one day notice her, and though it's been years, she couldn't help the giddiness she felt at finally being seen. Anaru Kahurangi had reached out to *her*. They were having a conversation.

*No one? I always assumed you'd be snatched up by some high-flying jet setter. You always were worlds above everyone else.*

Worlds above? Kate hardly thought so. She was intelligent, yes, but when it came to anything social, she felt awkward and out of her depth. Most of the time she preferred to stay out of it. It was easier than pretending to be something she wasn't and making a fool of herself.

A sting pierced her heart. Of course it was too good to be true. He had her confused with someone else. Someone more in his league.

*I think you have mistaken me for someone else. I was the one with her head stuck in a book all the time.*

*You always were funny* 😊

Now she knew he was wrong. She didn't have a funny bone in her body. And as far as she was aware, she'd never made anyone laugh before, not unless it was behind her back or at her expense.

*Maybe you're thinking of Kate Cassidy? She was... more outspoken.*

*If by outspoken you mean loud and obnoxious, yes she was. And no, I'm not talking about her. I know who you are, Kate Richardson. You showed me around the school on my first few days. You were top of almost every class we had together, and you were awarded Dux in our final year.*

Kate sat back, staring at her screen. She *had* done all those things.

*You pretty much kept to yourself, and I was too nervous to approach you back then.*

Kate blinked rapidly, rereading his last comment. *I was too nervous to approach you...* What did he mean *he* was too nervous? He was one of the most popular boys in school. He played in the first fifteen, excelled at athletics, and he'd even competed in an interschool cycle race and won. In what world was Anaru Kahurangi too nervous to approach *her*?

*Kate?*

*Sorry, I'm just in shock, I think. I didn't think you noticed me.*

*Oh, I noticed you alright. But I was just a jock, and you were way out of my league.*

Kate reached forward and grabbed the bottle of wine from the table, inspecting how much she'd had to drink. Only a few glasses. Not nearly enough to be hallucinating. She shook her head, letting it fall to the back of the couch so she could stare at the ceiling.

Every cell in her body longed for this to be real, but her brain wouldn't allow it. There had to be some mistake. They hadn't both been pining for the other and too scared to do anything about it; that would mean they'd wasted all these years. So much time that could have been theirs to share.

She swallowed the lump in her throat and forced her eyes back to the screen, scrolling back through the messages and rereading each one carefully.

There was no mistaking it. Even her always-searching-for-a-loophole brain had to agree. He felt for her what she felt for him. All this time, they'd been longing for each other and never knew.

Pulling her bottom lip between her teeth, she hovered her hands over the keyboard, trying to come up with the words to articulate how she felt.

**Did I say something wrong?**

*No. Never. I'm just trying to make sense of things.*

**I thought you knew.**

*How could I possibly have known that? We hardly said two words to each other.*

**Kate, I'm in construction. I work with my hands. Why would I have taken economics and history? I made sure to be in the classes you were in.**

***You really had no idea?***

*Not a clue. I can tell you, if I had known...*

Kate stopped herself, unsure how honest to be. This was the man who'd been in her every dream throughout high school and, if she was completely honest, college too. What she would give to turn the clock back. To have the chance to relive it all over again, only this time, unafraid of reaching out. How different would her life had turned out, she wondered. Would she have achieved all that she had if either of them had spoken up?

The ache inside her chest told her it would've been worth it, regardless. What good was a successful career and money if you had no one to share it with? Being at the top of her game all the time meant having very little social life. She lived and breathed her cases, giving her clients her all, but it was becoming increasingly clear, she'd missed out. She'd been so caught up in being the best, she didn't stop to actually live and enjoy the life she'd worked so hard for.

Inhaling a deep breath, she closed her eyes and stretched her neck side-to-side. It was time to take life by the balls and show it what she was made of. Time to give new meaning to her nickname.

*... if I had known, I would've told you I felt the same way about you.*

### ###

Kate blew into the office with an armload of files under her arm and a stern expression on her face. Claudia, her PA, fell into step beside her.

"How's my schedule for today? I need you to get hold of corrections and arrange a meeting with Kara Watson. I need to go over her statement again."

"Yes, Miss Richardson. I'll get right onto that." Claudia checked her notepad. "You've got a ten fifteen with Bobby Maguire, and a sit in with Jarod at eleven."

Kate nodded, brushing past Claudia's desk and straight through to her lavish corner office. "Okay, see if you can get me in with Kara late afternoon. That'll give me time to go over things with Jarod." She stopped at her desk, dropping the files into a tray. "Anything else?"

Claudia could barely contain her smile as she nodded. "They're waiting for you in conference room one."

Kate stifled a sigh as she lifted her head skyward. She should've known. "Okay, I'll be right there. Just give me a minute."

"Of course. I'll get onto that appointment for you." Claudia ducked out of the room, closing the door behind her.

"Jesus Christ," Kate hissed under her breath. Was it too much to ask that she be allowed to forget about Monroe Wilson and what he did? Even for one day?

Normally, she'd be all for celebrating the wins, but this one just felt wrong. She didn't want to celebrate her part in letting a brutal sex offender walk free. Her part in destroying that poor girl's life. She wanted to pretend the world was a better place than that. A place where women could wear what they want and go where they want without being judged and blamed for what some men assumed was their God given right.

She sucked in a breath, craning her neck side-to-side to work out the kinks that had found their way back as soon as she'd stepped foot in the office. For the first time in her career, she was having doubts about her future in this profession. Could she really sit back and allow these things to happen?

Beside her, the ping of a notification on her phone sounded, and she rifled through her bag to retrieve it. Anything to stall the undeserving accolades coming her way.

It was Anaru.

*Good morning. I was on my way to another job and drove past the old school. It made me think of you. Did you sleep okay?*

The corners of her lips tugged up and the tension she'd been feeling slowly dissipated. He'd been thinking of her.

*Better than I have in a long time. How about you? On your way to another job? That must've been an early start.*

**The life of a builder I'm afraid. Early starts and late finishes. But it's worth it to see the final product. You must get that too with your work.**

Kate huffed out a mirthless laugh. Defending people like Monroe was far from rewarding.

*Unfortunately, no. Quite the opposite in fact. I help people get away with the horrible things they've done.*

**But there must be some innocent folk in there. People you've really helped.**

She tried to remember the last time she legitimately believed her client's innocence. It had been far too few and much too long in between cases. That was never what she'd set out to do originally. She'd wanted to be the next RBG, working her way to the Supreme Court, but somewhere along the way she'd got lost; taken a wrong turn.

*Maybe one or two. Nothing like what you do. It must be so nice to have a hand in creating something spectacular every day. Making something out of nothing.*

*You make me sound far more interesting than I am. It's not all new builds and designs. I still have to crawl around under floors and in stinking hot roof spaces to lay insulation.*

*I suppose you're right. Every job has its ups and downs, and those on the outside never fully see it for what it is.*

**That was deep.**

*Lol I suppose it was. Don't mind me. I'm psyching myself up to receive adulations for something I feel is entirely unwarranted.*

**I don't believe anything you receive commendations for could be unwarranted. You must have done something impressive.**

*If by impressive you mean won a case that let a dangerous man back on the streets, then sure. I did that.*

Kate closed her eyes, knowing she would have to live with that for the rest of her life. If Monroe offended again, that would be on her.

**You were just doing your job, Kate. If it wasn't you defending him, it would've been someone else. Don't beat yourself up about it.**

*Except it wasn't anyone else, it was me. And at the risk of sounding completely arrogant and self-centred; no one else could've pulled it off. It was the unwinnable case.*

**That just proves how good you are at what you do.**

*What if I don't want to be good at that anymore?*

### 

By the end of the day, Kate was exhausted. She shut off her computer and pulled the door closed behind her, ready to leave. The nagging sensation she was neglecting something kept tugging at her chest, but she refused to give in. For once, she was going to forget about work for the weekend. The Watson case could wait until Monday, and Jarod had taken care of some of the smaller jobs that needed doing. So she was free to enjoy her weekend. Something she hadn't done in an eternity.

She had no plans, only the promise to herself that she would do some soul searching and work out what she really wanted out of life, because right now, her conscience was struggling with her life choices.

Kate had gone into law as an idealistic student wanting to change the world and follow in the greats' footsteps. She wanted to make a difference in the world, and in a way, she had. But what she'd done by giving Monroe Wilson the defence he paid for, would ultimately lead to another woman's demise. She knew as soon as he'd wrapped his sweaty arm around her that she'd made a mistake. That she was now part of the ongoing story of his deplorable behaviour, and there was nothing she could do about it.

Pulling into her drive, she was surprised to see a black van sitting in wait. Her mind instantly conjured images of Monroe Wilson hiding in the back, ready to grab her as she walked past. Her pulse quickened. Should she reverse out and drive as far away as possible? Call the cops? Or was this just her overactive imagination making something out of nothing?

It was too late to turn back. Whoever was in the van would've seen her already. So, she stopped the car, pulling the keys from the ignition. She took her time placing several between her fingers. If she was going down, she was going down with a fight.

With a shaky breath, she stepped out of the car. Her chin jutted out, she walked as stoically as she could muster towards the van. When she was almost level with the door, it swung open, and she held her keyed-up hand out in front of her.

"Whoa!" Anaru held his hands up, palms out. "It's just me."

Kate huffed out a breath, letting her hand fall to her side. "You scared me half to death! A little notice would've been nice." A nervous laugh fell from her lips. "What are you doing here?"

Anaru winced, bringing his hand up to scratch the back of his neck. "I'm sorry, I wasn't thinking. You, ah, sounded beat down in your messages, and I thought…" He shrugged. "I don't know. I thought maybe you could do with a hug?"

Kate's brows raised. "You drove all the way from Ashburton to give me a hug?"

"Uh, yeah." He held his arms out to his sides. "Is that weird?"

"A little, yeah." Kate grinned. "But it's also very sweet."

"That's what I was going for." He stepped forward. "Um, can I?" He opened his arms.

Kate stared at him, open mouthed. The boy she'd loved from afar was now the man standing before her, offering himself on a platter.

His hands lowered, and he shuffled his feet. "Uh… maybe I should've called first." He turned towards his van. "I'll just leave you to it. Sorry."

Kate blinked, then swallowed her nerves down. "No, wait!" She lunged forward, grabbing his wrist. "Don't go."

He turned towards her, and before she could think about it, she flung herself at him. His arms came up to rest on her back, pulling her in close. She rested her head on his chest, listening to his beating heart. It was strong and steady, like he was, and she felt safe. Secure.

Unbidden, tears pricked her eyes, and she couldn't stop them from falling down her cheeks in torrents. Years of pent-up emotion unleashed itself until she was sobbing, her hands clutching at his shirt.

Anaru held her tight, whispering, "It's okay. Let it all out. I've got you."

She cried until there was nothing left but a few hiccups, and his shirt was soaked through. Reluctantly, she pulled back, wiping her hand across the smear of makeup she'd left. "I'm sorry. I don't know what that was." She frowned, stepping away from him. "I've never… I don't even… What did you do to me?" She peered up at him in confusion. "I haven't cried in years. Haven't felt the need to. And then you show up and bam. It's like the Niagara Falls."

Anaru chuckled. "Is that a bad thing?"

"You tell me. Are you going to run for the hills as soon as I turn my back?" She laughed, but deep down, her heart lurched at the thought. She'd spent so many years trying to ignore her feelings for him, believing them to be unrequited, and now that he was here, standing in front of her… She couldn't imagine going back to a life without him in it. He was everything she'd been longing for, and she'd probably blown it straight off the bat.

Anaru cupped her jaw, his thumb wiping away the last remaining tears. "I'm not going anywhere. Not unless you tell me to."

"I don't want you to go," she whispered.

"Then I won't."

###

"Why don't you come to Ashburton for the night?" Anaru asked over coffee in the morning. "We could visit some of the old haunts, and you could take a proper break away from it all."

Kate's lips twisted to the side. It had been years since she'd been back there. After high school finished, she got as far away as she could, desperate to have a fresh start. After law school, she'd settled in Christchurch, only an hour's drive away, but she'd still never made the journey back. Ashburton held conflicting memories for her. It was a place where she excelled, but also a place she was ridiculed. It was where she'd fallen in love with Anaru, but also where she'd felt invisible. But perhaps going back with him by her side, it would be different.

"I suppose that might be nice."

"It's changed a lot over the years. You may find you like it." He grinned at her. "Take a step back from these high-end cases that have you tied in knots, and take on something different." He shrugged. "You never know."

Kate carried her mug to the sink and rinsed it, her shoulders bouncing as she laughed. "So that's what this is, is it? A ploy to get me to come back home?"

"That depends, is it working?" He arched a brow as he wrapped his hands around her waist.

"It might be."

"Then yes, it is a ploy. I want you all to myself, not up here where I can't see you every day." He leant forward, kissing her forehead.

"You move fast."

"Hey, I knew what I wanted years ago, and I let you get away. I'm not about to waste any more time that could be spent with you. Is that wrong?"

A warm glow filled her chest as she stretched up on tiptoes to wrap her arms around his neck. "It's definitely not wrong."

"So that's a yes? You'll come back with me?"

Kate chuckled, then pressed her lips to his. "It's a yes."

She didn't know what the future held for her in terms of her career, but she knew one thing for sure; wherever Anaru was, that's where she wanted to be.

*In 2024, I was meant to be at a book signing in Cardiff, but King Charles decided to get coronated that weekend, and the signing was postponed. Unfortunately, I had already booked out trip so could no longer attend the signing.*

*However, I had written this piece for the anthology to go with the signing, and now that the signing has been and gone, I can share it with you.*

# Fear of the Unknown

Stories and poems that prickle the senses.

# The Basement

"H…HELLO?  IS ANYBODY THERE?" Brandy called into the darkness. She fumbled with the light switch, flicking it up and down a few times before she remembered that it had blown last week, and she'd not yet replaced it. "Hello?" She took a cautious step forward, trailing her hand along the wall as she did so. "Who's there?" she called again, her voice catching in her throat. Her toe found the edge of the stairs leading down, and she inhaled a shaky breath before slowly descending.

There it was again. That scraping sound. Darting her eyes around the room, she tried to make out the shapes surrounding her, checking that nothing was out of place. She'd been in the basement a thousand times before, and she knew every inch of it. But the darkness combined with that eerie sound, played havoc with her senses. The air felt thick and she found herself bringing her hands to her neck, as if her sweater was strangling her. The hairs on the back of her neck began to prickle, a sudden chill running down her spine. Someone was down there with her.

The flick of a match to her right made her jump, clutching her hand to her chest. "Jesus, Joey! You scared the shit out of me!" she cried, balling her hands into fists and pummelling his upper arm.

"Hey, hey! Easy does it, Bran," he said with a laugh, holding his hands up in surrender. "I was just joking around."

"Ha ha, you're hilarious. I thought you were a murderer!"

"So, you came down to what? Hand yourself over? Babe," he grabbed her hips, pulling her into him, "I know you think you're a badass, but seriously, look at you. I could sneeze and you'd fly away." He chuckled, lowering his lips to brush against her ear. "You're much too delicate to be chasing after a killer."

"I'm not delicate," she whispered, finding it hard to concentrate with his body pressed against hers while they stood in the dark. She angled her neck, giving him better access as he began planting soft kisses on her bare skin. "Mmmmm," she moaned under her breath, spurring him on. Kissing along her jaw, he slowly slid his hand up her side, to cup her breast. "Joey," she said under her breath, "What are you doing here?"

He stopped short, his lips pressed just below her own. "Can't a guy visit his girlfriend on a Saturday night?" he asked, pulling away.

Folding her arms across her chest, Brandy stepped back. "Since when do you visit me in the basement?" she asked, her head cocked to the side.

"I was just..."

"You were trying to sneak in."

Rubbing his hand along the back of his neck, he laughed softly. "I was trying to surprise you."

"By climbing through my basement window and making creepy noises?"

"Creepy noises?"

"Come on, like it wasn't you making those scraping noises," she said, waiting for the joke to be revealed. Only Joey didn't answer her. Turning slowly, he backed up against her, fumbling for her hand. "Joey? You're scaring me," she said, the blackness surrounding them seeming to become even darker.

"Shhh," he hissed, holding his finger to his lips as he scanned the area in front of them. "Don't move." He pulled his box of matches from his pocket. A burst of light flickered for a second before blowing out, but it had been enough to see that they were not alone. Directly in front of them, had stood a man with hollow eyes, and a leering grin.

A piercing scream filled the room, bouncing off the walls and echoing back to them. It took a moment for Brandy to realise it was her screams permeating the air.

"Run!" Joey cried, pushing her towards the stairs. She scrambled blindly, trying to find her footing. Behind her, she could hear Joey lighting another match.

"Joey!" she screamed from halfway up the stairs. "Joey, where are you?" She continued backing up the stairway, her eyes riveted to the spot she had last seen him. "Joey?" she whimpered.

A whoosh of air hit her face as something large thudded in front of her feet. With shaking hands, she reached forward, her fingers finding purchase on something soft and wet. Raking her fingers back and forth in the dampness, she found a chain with a smooth metal heart attached. With her heart pounding, she pulled it closer, swiping her hands across the metal to feel for an engraving. She couldn't see it, but she would know it anywhere. Engraved on each side, were initials. JC and BR. Joey Chambers and Brandy Rose.

Swallowing back a sob, Brandy reached forward once again, her fingers brushing along the softness in front of her. A tiny box protruding from the mound, caused her to pause. She eased it out of its enclosure. With trembling fingers, she struck a match, instantly regretting it. Her mouth dropped open, an anguished scream bursting forth as she sat there, staring at the body of her boyfriend, with his severed head staring up at her.

*This story came to me in a dream. I woke in a sweat after seeing the whole thing play out in my head. I don't know what I'd been watching or reading that night, but I had two very vivid dreams that creeped me out. The other one I'm yet to write about, but it is still firmly planted in my mind. Perhaps one day I'll explore where that one will go.*

***This one was turned into a novella called "Mine" and is part of my Dark Sins Novellas.***

# Betrayal

I GIVE THE SIGNAL, and everyone crouches low, our ears straining in the deafening silence as we listen for the sound that came from outside the boarded-up window. The sound I'm sure was a footstep.

I should've known it was too good to be true, this place we'd come to think of as home. We'd been lucky to have stumbled across it all those months ago as we barely clung to life. We'd barely escaped the blast that killed half our men and left us broken and defeated, mere shells of the people we once were.

All we wanted was some shelter to live out our numbered days before the flesh-eaters found us and we became another number amongst the lifeless souls that wandered the earth.

But that day never came.

With night falling upon us, we trudged into this deserted house and never stepped foot outside again.

The bomb shelter below had enough food and supplies to last us years, and with our malnourished bodies finally filled, we had set about protecting what was now ours. Windows and doors were boarded, alarms were set around the perimeter, and barricades were in place. We made this place an impenetrable fortress.

Until it wasn't.

We trusted too easily. Even after all our heartache, we still held on to the hope that deep down, people were good.

He'd been no more than ten years old when he collapsed against our door, begging for a place to stop for the night. We took pity on the kid who looked as weak as a kitten with his bandy legs. After all, how could one child bring down the family we had built?

Micah became one of us, pitching in with chores, taking his turn to keep watch at night. He fit in well with our little family, and we let our guards down. *I* let my guard down. I let him in, this boy with eyes the same almond shape as my own.

It had been my decision to throw him out with two broken legs and nothing to defend himself against the wolves that waited. After what he'd done, he deserved a fate much worse than death. He deserved to be eaten alive, listening to the sounds of his own screams as he was slowly devoured by the walking dead.

A month has passed since the day I lost my last shred of humanity. Now, perched against the wall, I am prepared to fight tooth and nail to protect what is mine. I signal for the others to ready their weapons as I hear the sound once again. This time I'm positive it's a footstep. Sure and steady, not like the walkers who roam aimlessly looking for their next meal.

A white-hot flame erupts, hitting me square in the back, lighting my entire body as I jolt forward, watching splinters of wood and glass fly past me in slow motion. My body lands with a thud and heat envelopes me until I can no longer move. All I can do is stare at the gaping mouths of my family and hope they know how much I love them, even if I didn't show it. But shock quickly turns to fear as they look past me, beyond the flames ripping through my body and our once-safe haven. And I know without a doubt who has their attention. The same one responsible for the blast that killed our men. The same one who broke my heart with his betrayal. The same one with the bandy, broken legs. The only one who could defeat us. Micah, the one I called my son.

*I'd been struggling to finish the story I originally started for this topic, but when I awoke in a sweat after a nightmare where I'd broken the legs of a kid during a zombie apocalypse, I knew I had my story. So, at three in the morning, I grabbed my phone and quickly wrote it down – but not as it happened in the dream, but what happened after.*

*I'm almost tempted to turn this one into a novel as well. I'll have to add it to my neverending list of story ideas!*

# Night Terrors

I MUST BE IMAGINING THINGS. Or perhaps it's a dream? Surely that must be it. I can't possibly be hearing the duelling banjos at three in the morning. No one in their right mind would crank that up at this ungodly hour. Or *any* hour, for that matter.

Reaching a hand out to the wall, I knock three times. "Can you keep it down please?"

The music quiets, and I nestle back under my sheets, my eyes already closing. I get maybe thirty seconds of peace before it's shattered by a piercing rendition of *Achy Breaky Heart.* Whoever is singing sounds as though they've stood on a bag of cats. It's awful.

"Please can you turn it down? I have an early start in the morning," I call, trying to appeal to their empathetical nature. I should've known it wouldn't work. You can't appeal to something that isn't there.

Something drags across the floor until it hits the wall, and that's when the banjo starts up again only this time it's a real-life rendition, not a recording. Before long, someone starts clapping and stamping their feet in time, adding a hearty "Yeeha!" for good measure.

"Ugh!" I lift my pillow and hold it over my ears. Squeezing my eyes shut, I will my mind to block out all the noise and go to sleep.

***

A thud followed by footsteps jolts me from my slumber. Noting the time, I roll out of bed and pad to the bathroom.

All is quiet next door, and I'm tempted to do something loud just to spite them, but my inner voice convinces me otherwise. Instead, I make my way to the kitchen for some much-needed caffeine. Leaning against the counter, I peer out the window, watching for any signs of life. There's a flicker of movement before the door swings open and they step out into the morning sunshine. They even have the nerve to look rested too. How dare they?

Slamming my mug down on the bench, I stalk to my door and fling it open, my arms folding across my chest as I step out to greet them with narrowed eyes.

"Izzy! You're awake!" She smiles as if butter wouldn't melt.

"No thanks to you," I mumble.

"You seem a little tired." Her eyes glisten with a glee I want to wipe off her face.

"I wonder why that might be." I quirk an eyebrow. They say kids should come with an instruction manual, but if you ask me, it's the parents who need one.

Mum takes Dad's hand and they bounce down the steps with a laugh. She always warned me they'd make sure I understood how it felt when I gave them sleepless nights as a moody teen. I never expected them to follow through, though.

Payback's a bitch.

*Whenever my kids drive me insane, my mum often tells me it's payback for the terror I was as a child, so I figured why not write a story about parents getting their own back?*
*When I was a youngster in my first flat, the concrete walls separating flats sometimes seemed non-existent. I could hear every time they made a coffee or played music. And I actually did hear duelling banjos one night! Ah the good ol' days.*

# Skin Deep

## Cassidy

## 1991

"DON'T YOU THINK YOU'VE HAD ENOUGH, Cassidy?" Her eyes narrow as she scrutinises the half-eaten candy bar in my hand. "You don't want to get fat now, do you?"

"No, Mum," I whisper, tucking the rest of the bar back inside the wrapper and stowing it in my drawer.

"You know I'm just looking out for you. I worry." She places my folded laundry on the bed and sits down. Her eyes soften slightly before landing on my stomach with a sigh. "You're already a little soft around the edges. It can be hard to lose it once it's there, trust me, I know." She pats her flat stomach as if to say she too was once a little fluffy like me, but I've seen the photos; she has always been a waif.

I nod, knowing she won't stop until I agree to try harder. My fingers thread together as I lower my gaze to my belly. Is it really so bad to be a little pudgy? Don't they call it puppy fat because it goes away as you get older? Or am I bigger than I think? I chance a glance at my mother, her pursed lips and look of disgust tell me that maybe I am. So big that a candy bar is frowned upon, that's for sure.

My eyes flit between the flat expanse of her abdomen and the pudgy protuberance of my own, and I wonder, not for the first time, why I couldn't be more like her. Sure, I like to eat candy, but so does every other 13-year-old girl I know. I play netball, go for walks, and I love to dance, so it's not for a lack of trying. But when I look at her, I see the lithe body of a ballerina, and then there's me, with the body of a sumo wrestler minus the nappy.

Mum keeps talking, something about diets, but I zone out, seeking the photos on my wall for reassurance. The ones I took with my friends only a few weeks ago at the school dance.

Reassuring, they are not. I've always known I was bigger than them, but for the first time I see myself through my mother's eyes, and I don't like it. The subtle differences seem to stand out so much more in our party dresses; the way the fabric clings to my body that little bit more, the way I bulge around the straps. Suddenly the pictures no longer remind me of a fun night with my friends, but make me see myself in a new light, and it's unflattering.

I vow to myself to make more of an effort. To exercise more and eat less. To make myself look normal. Like everyone else.

### 

# Cassidy

# Present day

"Jenna Adams?" I smile as the reserved brunette stands, tucking her hair behind her ear as she trails behind her mother. "Mrs Adams?" I hold my hand out to her. "I'm Cassidy Rae, a mental health nurse. We spoke on the phone."

"Yes." Her lip trembles as her eyes begin to water. "Thank you for seeing us on such short notice. I wasn't sure what else to do." She curls a protective arm around her daughter's shoulders before taking a seat.

"You did the right thing to call. We're here to help." I turn to Jenna. "Do you know why you're here?"

She glances at her mother before nodding her head. "Yeah," she whispers.

I smile reassuringly. "This is a safe place, okay? You're not in trouble, we just want to see if we can help you deal with some of these feelings you've been having."

She ducks her head, her fingers digging into the soft flesh of her thigh as she mumbles, "Mhmm."

"Your mum tells me you've been having some pretty big conversations with your friends. Talking about things that maybe scared them a little."

Her head bobs up and down.

"What your friends did? Telling an adult? It may seem like a betrayal to you, but they did it because they're worried about you, okay? They want to make sure you get the help you need so you don't have to go through this alone." I take a breath, giving her a chance to absorb my words. "Can you tell me how long you've been feeling this way?"

Her shoulders lift in a shrug. "A while, I guess." Her eyes flick towards her mum who is sniffling. Swiping a box of tissues from my desk, I hold them out to her.

"Thank you." She dabs at her eyes. "Sorry."

"There's no need to apologise. All emotions are valid. I know this probably came as a shock to you."

Her face crumples and fresh tears pool in her eyes as she nods her head. "I had no idea."

"Jenna, how does that make you feel? To see your mum upset like this?" I lean forward, resting my elbows on my knees.

Again, she shrugs. "Bad."

"Bad?"

"She's sad because of me. It's my fault." Her fingers move frantically in her lap, picking at her skin as if she needs to inflict pain on herself. I reach out and place my hand on hers.

"It's not your fault that she's sad, honey." I wait until she looks up, meeting my eyes. "You can't control how she feels. Yes, she's sad, but it's because she's probably a little scared, confused, and above all else, I'd say she's very worried."

She shakes her head, turning to stare at the wall.

"I *am* worried about you, Jenna," Mrs Adams starts. "I wish you felt like you could come to me, that I didn't have to hear it from the school… that you've been… you've been… talking about…" her voice drops to a whisper, "…suicide."

Jenna's knee bobs up and down as she twists her body even further around in the seat. She lifts her thumb to her lips, chewing at the edges.

"Can you tell me what you've been saying to your friends, Jenna? Why they felt compelled to reach out?"

The silence stretches out a beat before she replies. "Just that no one would miss me. That sometimes I wish it was over; that it would end."

"And by 'it' you mean?"

She turns her wide brown eyes on me. "Life."

### 

# Cassidy

## 1992

I stand in front of the bathroom mirror in my birthday suit, trying to decide if I look any smaller yet. It's only been a few months, but I've been trying really hard to eat smaller meals and be more active. My stomach seems to be in a constant state of hunger, forever grumbling and embarrassing me in front of my friends, but if it will get me to be skinny like them, it's a price I'm willing to pay.

I poke a finger into my stomach and watch everything shake when I pull it out. I twist and turn, trying to find an angle that is even a tiny bit more flattering, but everywhere I turn, I look the same.

Chunky. That's what Toni had called me when I'd asked if I could try on her new top. She said it wouldn't fit me because I'm a little chunky and she didn't want me to stretch it. I know she didn't mean anything by it, but it still hurt. I laughed it off, even letting them use it as a nickname for the rest of the day, when inside I was crying like a baby.

I just want to be like everyone else. I want to wear swimming togs without looking lumpy, and to look good in a tank top. I want to wear those short skirts without my thighs rubbing together. I want boys to notice me, the way they do Toni and all my other friends. I want to be able to sit down without worrying if I've got rolls hanging over my pants.

What's wrong with me that I can't lose the weight? I don't understand. I'm trying so hard, but nothing is working. There's loose skin and squishy bits all over my hips and thighs, and my arms have these dangly bits that wobble when I wave. I don't know what I'm doing wrong. Everyone around me seems to be getting skinny and shapely, while I'm just one big shape. Round.

###

# Cassidy

## Present day

My head falls back as I sink into the soft cushion of the staffroom couch. Sometimes my job can be rewarding, and other days, it just plain sucks. Today is one of those days.

*Life*.

Jenna's voice keeps echoing in my head, reminding me what a dysfunctional world we live in. Depression stats are on the rise, and our country's mentality is to 'toughen up' and 'get over it'. It's no wonder we have young girls like Jenna considering taking their own life.

Thirteen. The same age I was when I first started having body image issues, and I'm not blind to the fact that girls of today have it worse. In this world of social media where everyone is judged on their selfies and how many likes they have, it's not hard to see how things can escalate. All it takes is one negative comment, one person to start up a tyrannical rant, and suddenly you're attacked on your choices. It's one giant popularity competition that no one ever really wins.

I squeeze my eyes shut and huff out a sigh.

"You're thinking about her again, aren't you?" Kym opens her locker, grabbing her handbag and jacket.

"Yeah." I pinch the bridge of my nose between my thumb and finger. "I just wish there was something more I could do. Something to make her see that she's got so much to live for, you know?" I peer up at her, dropping my hand to my lap. "I just want her to know things get better. High school isn't the be all and end all of life, you know?"

Perching on the coffee table, she opens her bag, pulling out a small box of chocolates. "I know that, but she's a teenager, and they can't think beyond high school." She rests her hand on my knee. "You know how this works. You're helping her just by being here to talk to. You always get through to them one way or another." She opens the box and holds it out to me. "Chocolate?"

My mouth salivates by the mere mention of the word, and I get a whiff of the sweetness as she waves the box under my nose.

"Go on. Chocolate makes everything better."

*If only that were true.*

I look down at my stomach then back up to the box. *What the hell. It's only one.*

### 

One turned into an entire box and then some.

Having that miniscule taste was enough to send me straight to the supermarket on my way home from work. I bought a big box of chocolates and a tub of ice cream to wash it down with. Restraint has never been my strong point.

Now, I'm sitting in front of the TV, watching the credits roll along the screen, surrounded by candy wrappers and a half-eaten tub of melting ice cream. I feel horrific. My stomach is both queasy and bloated, and I think I'm breaking out in dairy sweats, if that's even a thing.

Why do I do this to myself? Why can't I have more self-control?

I scoop up the offending wrappers, desperate to get rid of them. Out of sight, out of mind. Into the bin they go.

Dusting my hands down my pants, I peer over at the tub of ice cream, and even though my stomach is roiling, the thoughts still pop into my head. *Just one more taste.* My subconscious isn't always my friend. Taunting me, trying to lure me into that bad place again. The place we vowed never to go to again.

*But it's so good.*

I can't help myself. The tub is in my hand before I even realise what I'm doing. My fingers slick with the creamy dessert as I make a spoon with my hand and scoff the rest of the tub. I don't even sit back down, just stand there, eating like a kid who's never had candy before. I don't stop until my fingers scrape the bottom. And I know, it's only just the beginning.

###

# Cassidy

## 1993

"Ugh, I can't eat another bite." Toni pushes her plate away, leaving a half-eaten slice of pizza. I look down at my empty plate and follow suit.

"Me either." I hungrily stare at the pizza box; the glistening cheese whispering promises of its deliciousness. No more for me though. Not if I want to fit into those size ten jeans I bought today. As it is, I can barely pull the zipper up, let alone move in them. I've got a little more weight to lose to fit them. Toni suggested they could be my 'goal pants'. She said her mum does that whenever she's dieting and trying to lose weight. I've always thought her mum was beautiful, so if it works for her, it's bound to work for me.

Toni wipes her hands on a napkin then drags her shopping bag closer, pulling out a cute dress and holding it against her body. "What do you think?" She does a twirl on the spot, the fabric flying out around her. "Do you think Jason will like it?"

I study my friend, taking in her long, slim legs, flat stomach, and just the right amount of curve to her hips. She's gorgeous. "He'd be crazy not to like you in it. I bet he'd still like you even if you were in a sack." I sigh, letting my hands fall into my lap. I'd kill to have just one boy look at me the way Jason looks at her.

"Hey." Toni sits beside me, throwing her arm around my shoulder. "You'll get a boyfriend soon. I can feel it." She leans across and snags the jeans from my bag. "Especially once you get into these babies! They won't know what's hit them."

I know she's trying to make me feel better, but why can't they notice me for me and not what my body looks like in a pair of jeans that cut off my circulation? Why does being beautiful have to be so hard? The women in the magazines make it look so easy. I'd probably have to starve myself to look like them, but I like food too much to do that. If only there was a way I could still eat everything I want without putting on the extra weight. A girl can dream, I guess.

### ###

# Cassidy

# Present Day

"Thank you for coming back to see me, Jenna. It's very brave of you."

She shifts in her seat, pulling her lip between her teeth. "Whatever."

I rest my elbows on my knees and press my hands together. "I mean it. Asking for help is the first step to recovery, and it takes a lot of guts to come forward like that."

She stares at a spot behind my head as her fingers slowly pick at the skin around her wrists. "I didn't ask for your help," she mutters.

"You're still here though."

She huffs again, meeting my eyes briefly before nodding towards the door. "Only because she's making me."

"Your mother?" The roll of her eyes is all the answer I'm going to get from her. "You know it's because she cares, right? She wants what's best for you, and what you're doing to yourself isn't really what's best, is it?" I wait her out, letting my words sink in. If there's anything I know about young girls, it's that they may not show it outwardly, but they take everything in.

Her eyes remain focused on the wall above my head and her fingers begin pulling at the already tattered fabric on the sleeve of her top. "What are you feeling right now, Jenna?"

"That this is stupid, and I don't want to be here." She finally meets my eyes, and I can see the pain she's trying to hide.

"And by here you mean?"

She lifts her arm in a small arc. "Here."

"Okay. I can understand that. You probably think that I don't know what I'm talking about, right? That I wouldn't understand how you're feeling?"

Tears fill her eyes as she turns away, finding a poster of a kitten hanging from a branch with the words *Hang in there* above it. "No one understands."

I nod, leaning back in my chair. I know that feeling all too well. "Here's what I think. You're feeling some strong and confusing emotions and you don't know what to do with them. Sometimes it can feel like you're all alone and that no one else could possibly feel what you're feeling." A frown forms on her face; the only sign she's listening. "Sometimes it can feel as though everything is out of control, and that can be scary. Self-harm is a way of taking back some of that control." I nod at where her fingernails are gouging into the soft flesh of her palm. She stops, tugging on the hem of her sleeve to cover the red welts forming.

My heart hurts for her, and it takes all my focus not to reach out and pull her into my arms. When you're in a place where you feel as though no one understands you, it can be the loneliest place in the world. Knowing that someone, just one person, gets it can be all the difference sometimes, but it can also be the spiral that pushes them further if you're not careful.

"The thing with self-harming, though, is that it's only a temporary 'fix'. It might make those overwhelming feelings go away for a little while, but then they come back, don't they?"

She shrugs, seeming to sink back into herself more.

"It can also become a habit that's hard to break, and sometimes that can lead to you hurting yourself more than you'd planned."

"Maybe that's the point," she whispers.

"Why do you say that?"

"Because I'm useless." She brings her thumb to her lips and begins to chew the barely-there nail.

"Why do you think you're useless, Jenna?"

She turns her pained stare to me. "Because I'm fat and ugly, and nobody likes me." She holds my gaze, almost as if she's challenging me to say differently.

"I like you."

She snorts, shaking her head. "You have to say that. But you don't even know me."

"I know you better than you think."

###

# Cassidy

# 1994

I brace my hands on the cool porcelain as I take in a shaky breath and close my eyes. My stomach muscles clench tight, convulsing twice more before settling. I lean back on my haunches, swiping some toilet paper from the roll to dab at my mouth and wipe my fingers. At least I didn't get it all over myself this time.

Standing, I press the button to flush and watch my dinner swirl down the drain, making sure every last bit of evidence is gone before I walk to the basin to wash my hands. I catch my reflection in the mirror.

My eyes automatically go to the rounded protrusion of my belly and the extra padding that's suddenly appeared on my hips. I'm what they call a "late bloomer", though what I've bloomed is even less desirable than the original.

With my fingers and thumb, I pinch the flesh I hate so much, despised by how much still lingers. No matter how much I purge myself, the weight won't budge, and I continue to expand.

Sucking my cheeks in and holding my breath as tight as I can, I turn this way and that, inspecting every inch of my disgusting body. I can barely stand to look at myself, but I force my eyes to continue their scrutiny, picking out every imperfection I need to work on. Too much of this and not enough of that. It's no wonder guys don't even look in my direction when I can barely stomach my own reflection.

I let out my breath and watch as my belly sags back to its dismal position. My shoulders hunch, and I clench my fists as a hatred so pure roils in the pit of my stomach. I'm loathsome. Vile. Unlovable.

A sob breaks free from my chest as I let those words simmer in my brain. My eyes squeeze tight, and before I know what I'm doing, my fist connects with the mirror, distorting my image to something even more grotesque. But it's the feeling of release that sings through my veins as I watch blood drip from my knuckles and swirl down the drain that grabs me and holds me tight. That fleeting moment as glass pierces my skin, sucking away the anger and disgust I held towards myself only moments ago, and all I feel is relief.

### 

# Cassidy

# Present Day

My fingers trail the puckered flesh on my ribs just below my bra line as I stare at the tub of vanilla ice cream I just polished off and brought back up. That's three weeks in a row I've devoured more food than should be humanly possible, only for it to end up down the drain minutes later. How did I end up back in the place I fought so hard to get out of?

I've always taken pride in the fact I was able to pull myself out from that dark place, that abyss that tried so hard to take me down but failed. I went to university. I trained to become the person who could be that strength for others when they couldn't find it within themselves, and yet here I am, right back where it all began.

I find the long ridge that runs along my left side; the one that went too deep and too far. The one that nearly killed me but became my saving grace. I've always thought of it as my battle scar. A reminder of how I fought my demons and came out on the other side a stronger person. But all it took was a girl not dissimilar to myself when I was her age. A girl who brought back all those insecurities I fought so hard to overcome; a girl who felt her life was worth so little because she didn't fit the perfect mould of society.

*Fat. Ugly. Useless.*

How many times had I told myself those very same words over the years?

*Unlovable. Loathsome. Disgusting.*

How many more times will I continue telling myself today?

With silent tears running down my face, I take a deep, shaky breath, knowing what comes next. The blade I'd brought back with me from the bathroom glints from the edge of the table. I know all I have to do is reach out and grab it, and the pain I feel inside will go away.

*Just reach out and take it.*

I close my eyes and see that girl standing in front of the shattered mirror as her anguish washed away alongside her blood. I see her and I feel that elation coursing through her body until the shock subsides and she's left with an empty, hollow feeling that was worse than before. I see her, and I realise there's only one thing left to do.

Reaching out, I drag it closer to the edge of the table. My eyes blur with fresh tears, but I blink them away, determined to see it through. With a caress so gentle, I bring it to my ear and hold my breath, counting the ticking of the clock on the wall.

*One... two... three...*

"Hello?"

"Kym? It's Cassidy." *Deep breath.* "I... I need your help."

Skin Deep *was a story I started writing a few years ago. It was originally going to be part of an anthology, but I decided to go another route, and this one just sat around waiting for me to pick it back up again.*

*I had planned on turning it into a full length, but then I entered it in a competition here in New Zealand instead. I don't think it needs to be full length to get the point across. It's powerful in its simplicity.*

# Getting Dirty

Droplets trail down my windowpane
As big grey clouds cry tears of rain.
I watch and wonder how it came to be;
Mother Nature so in tune with me.
I press my face against the glass,
And ponder how long it will last.
Perhaps the sun will clear the gloom
Both in the yard and in my room.
I close my eyes and will it so,
And then outside is where I'll go.
Out to where the flowers sway
Against the tapestry of grey.
I'll dance my way through fields of green,
And let the sun wipe my slate clean.
I blink my eyes to see
The universe listened to me.
Rain falls no more from the sky.
The sun is peaking through up high.
A smile forms upon my lips
As out the door I do skip…
Straight into a puddle of mud
Where I land with a great big thud.
I try to stand but slip back down
As mud squelches all around.

It's in my hair and up my nose;
It's even gone between my toes.
The wet and cold seeps through my skin,
But instead of rage, I simply grin.
Perhaps the best way to rid a funk
Is to slip around in a puddle of gunk.

Getting Dirty *was written for an assignment of the same name. We were challenged to write a poem about getting dirty in the mud. I found this one difficult to write at first, but once I let the emotion take over, it all seemed to flow.*

# I am the Glitch

I BLINK MY EYES OPEN, and I'm met with a crinkled sheet of paper folded in half and propped against my alarm clock. My name is scrawled across the front in suspiciously familiar handwriting.

Pulling myself up, I wipe the sleep from my eyes as I scan the room. Nothing else seems out of place, just this well-worn sheet of paper.

With shaking hands, I grasp it, slowly peeling the corner and flattening the page across my lap, and suddenly I'm hit with an overwhelming sense of déjà vu.

*Sammy,*

*Right now, you're wondering where this letter came from and who left it here. The simple answer is, you did. You see, your life is in a never-ending loop, and you're doomed to watch everyone you love disappear over and over again. No matter how many times you try to fix it, it always ends the same; an apocalyptic explosion.*

*You, Sammy, are a glitch in the matrix. An error. Your very presence is what causes the end of the world as you know it, and only you can stop it from happening again. In a moment, I, that is, future you, will appear in the doorway with a map. You must follow the new coordinates in red and find Maximus. I believe he is the key to ending this vicious cycle and returning the world to rights.*

I let the paper fall from my hands as I stare unseeing at the wall. My mind tries to piece it all together, but deep down, I know this letter speaks the truth. I've never truly felt like I belong.

With dread sitting heavily in my stomach, I reach for the drawer beside my bed, knowing what I have to do. A tear rolls down my cheek as I hold the blade in both hands, angled towards my abdomen. I let my mind conjure images of my mother's smiling face and Carrie's emerald-green eyes. I try to imprint them in my brain so I can carry them with me to whatever plain I wind up on. Taking one final breath, I close my eyes and—

"Sammy, stop!"

Just as the letter said, a wary-looking version of myself stands in the doorway, his arm extended towards me as if the very action can stop what must be done.

"I know you think this will make it all end, but it doesn't. You've tried it a million times already. You can't die, because I already exist. You need to go back to the beginning and make it so you never existed in the first place."

I shake my head, my eyes falling to the blade still held firm in my grasp.

*I am the glitch.*

I plunge the blade into my stomach, hearing the distant cries of my older self as I fall into darkness.

I blink my eyes open, and I'm met with a crinkled sheet of paper folded in half and propped against my alarm clock. My name is scrawled across the front in suspiciously familiar handwriting.

I am the Glitch *was a fun assignment where we had to write a letter to our younger selves. Instead of taking the usual route of writing an inspirational type of letter to uplift my younger self, I was inspired to write this darker piece after watching a foreign series on Netflix called* Dark.

# The Plan

AN ALARM SOUNDS, and I blink my eyes open with a start. The room is so dark I can barely make out my hand in front of my face. A tap drips in a room close by, and there's a stale smell of mildew in the air.

"Hello?" My voice croaks as if I haven't used it in a long time, and I'm hit with a sense of foreboding.

The alarm goes off again, and a tiny light shines from across the room as a phone dances over the tabletop. I swing my legs down from where I lay, testing the ground beneath my feet before making a move towards the phone.

Snatching it up, I'm met with an unknown number on the screen and a message that reads, "Meet me outside."

With a frown, I dismiss the message, placing the phone back on the table and scanning the room around me as my eyes adjust to the dark. Nothing about this place seems familiar, and I can't seem to recall why I'm here.

The phone lights up with another message. This time it's one word. "Now."

I stagger towards the sliver of light coming from a gap in the curtains and shift the fabric enough that I can see outside. A hooded figure stands with his back to the house and a large bag in hand. My heart pounds and my breath quickens. Something tells me this person is not to be messed with.

On shaky legs, I stumble out the door and down the path, my eyes darting side to side. I'm still none the wiser as to my whereabouts or how I got here. The street is quiet with houses on either side. A car rests on blocks up the road a little, and at least half the streetlights are broken. Even the moon is in hiding, covered almost completely by clouds.

I reach the man, shoving my hands in my pockets and clearing my throat. He keeps watch over the street, not bothering to look at me as he says, "It's done."

My stomach ties in knots. "What is?"

"Exactly." He drops the bag by his feet and steps away. "Everything you need is in here. Wait for dawn to break then hop on the bus. Ticket's inside."

I open my mouth to speak, but he holds his hand up, stopping me. "It's all in there." He nods towards the bag then turns on his heels and strides away.

I snatch the bag from the ground and rush back inside, away from the dancing shadows and unfamiliar street. Dumping the bag on the table, I use the torch on my phone to look it over. Plain black, nondescript, large enough to carry a weeks' worth of clothes, but not so big it could contain a dead body. Strangely though, that thought does little to calm my nerves.

Inhaling a deep breath through my nose and huffing it out through my mouth, I slowly unzip the bag.

Inside is everything I imagine you'd need to start a new life. A passport and driver's license with my picture on them and a name I don't recognise. A change of clothes, a black wig cut in a short bob, and a wad of cash. Tucked into the side pocket is the bus ticket with my new name printed on it. One way to Invercargill.

I slump down onto the couch, staring at the contents of the bag. A recipe for disaster if ever I saw one. What am I running from? What happens when I get to Invercargill? And why the hell can't I remember anything?

Tipping the bag upside down, I give it a shake. A small sheet of folded paper floats to the floor. I stoop down to pick it up, using my phone light to read the flowing handwriting.

*Lexie,*

*You won't remember, but this is your plan. The effects should wear off in the morning, and you will be right as rain. The main thing is, it worked. Massimo believes you to be dead.*

*Everything has been arranged. Zeke will meet you at the bus station in Invercargill. You can trust him. He will look after you.*

*You will board the Queen Elizabeth at the end of the week, and then you're home free. Keep your head down until then.*

*Do not, under any circumstances, tell anyone your real name. From now on, you are Svetlana Petrov, a Russian tourist. We can't risk Massimo finding out. It'll be my head if he does.*

*Good luck.*

*Bethany.*

I scrunch my eyes closed as I massage my temples. I know it's in there somewhere. A flash of angelic blonde hair and ice-blue eyes dances in my mind, and I remember. Bethany was my friend. A maid of sorts, but my friend all the same. My fingers lift to the tender spot below my ear, and I wince. At night, Bethany would sit with me and braid my hair to cover the bruises. She would tend to my wounds and whisper softly to me. She was my friend, and she helped me escape the brutal hands of my father.

The Plan *is actually two writing assignments combined. The first half was one where we had to write about receiving a text from an unknown number saying, "Meet me outside. Now." The second half was an assignment that needed to include a recipe in it, so I figured I'd give the original piece an ending while creating a recipe for disaster.*

# The List

THE SCREAMS ARE DEAFENING behind me, but no matter how hard I try, I can't seem to make myself turn around. It would make it too real. No. It's better to close my eyes and pretend I'm anywhere else in the world, and not here, attempting to face my fears and do something I've always wanted to do but been too scared to.

A hand reaches out and takes mine, giving a squeeze. "You ready?" Michelle yells over the din, and I shake my head.

"Not yet. Just give me a minute."

"Come on. You've got this, babe. Just close your eyes and don't think about it. Be in the moment." She tugs my arm higher, as if she's about to dive into the depths of the ocean, dragging me with her.

I swallow the ball of dread in the back of my throat and shuffle back until my heels are teetering over the edge. I remind myself there are bigger things to be afraid of. Things beyond my control.

A matter of months, that's what they'd said. The cancer had struck hard and fast, and at the behest of my best friend, I made a bucket list of all the things I'd never had a chance to do, and one by one, we've been ticking them off the list before I shuffle off this mortal coil.

"Okay." I nod. "I'm ready."

"On the count of three. One…"

I raise my other arm up high.

"… two…"

I throw my head back and stare at the twinkling stars in the sky.

"… three!"

With a hoarse scream, I bend my knees and throw my body backwards into the crowd, with Michelle by my side. What feels like hundreds of hands take hold of my body, guiding me as I glide through the night. I don't know them, and they don't know me, but there is a silent agreement between us, assuring me I'll be looked after. They won't let me fall.

Music thrums through my veins and a bubble of giddy laughter bursts from my lips. "I did it!" I scream into the sky, and an eruption of whistles and cries fill the air around me.

*I did it.*

Tears fill my eyes as emotion overwhelms me. This leap of faith was the last thing to be ticked off.

My days may be numbered, but my list is complete.

The List *was an assignment titled "Leap of Faith". Originally, I was planning on going down the humorous route, but then this story kind of took over. Yes, it's sad, but it's also a reminder to face those fears and live your best life. Make sure you chase those dreams of yours.*

# Dreamcatcher

CROUCHING IN THE CORNER OF THE ROOM, Azriel watched the rhythmic up and down motion of the child's breath as she slept. She seemed at peace this evening, unlike the past few nights of her sentry. Terrible nightmares had plagued the child since her father's passing, and it was Azriel's duty to watch over her.

Fluttering eyelashes and a tiny whimper escaped the child's lips as she rolled to her side. It was beginning.

Azriel took her place on the edge of the bed, her hands braced gently over the child's head. She closed her eyes, concentrating as the child tossed and turned. Her hands heated as she caught the bad dream and drew each strand from the child's mind. Wisps curled around her fingers, searching for an escape, but Azriel was careful, ensuring every last piece made it into the dream net strapped to her side. If even the slightest remnant remained, it could cause the child to have what was called a dayscare, and they were much harder to catch.

The child's breathing evened out, and the crinkles in her face smoothed. Her eyelids fluttered gently as she returned to the hypnotic dreamscape

Azriel had planted; a field of poppies and tulips dancing in the wind, and her father walking beside her, hand-in-hand. A smile graced the child's lips as she sighed and rolled over, tucking her hands beneath her head. She would sleep in peace now.

Azriel pulled the dream net tight, twisting the top to secure the nightmare inside. It was a long journey back to the Land of Nod, where Dreamcatchers wove their magic on the horrifying visions conjured in the minds of children, and Azriel had already stayed well past her time.

With a click of her fingers, she vanished from her spot beside the child, reappearing in the shadows outside her window. Travelling through the shadow realm was the fastest way home, but it was also the most dangerous. As a young catcher, she had been warned of the Snarlers that hid amongst the darkness, waiting for the few who ventured out of the light and into shadow. They fed off nightmares, gaining strength with each one.

But if Azriel was to make it home before daybreak, she would need to do just that. With a quick glance over her shoulder, she faded into the empty void, wading through the thick fog clinging to her legs and clawing at her arms. Tendrils whirled about, lifting her hair and whispering in her ear. A shiver ran down the back of her neck as she shook them off. She focused all her energy on dispelling the coldness seeping through her clothes and into her flesh. It would not take hold of her or her dream net, of that she was sure. Leaning forward, she trudged through the heavy air, kicking the icy fingers of despair from around her ankles. Only a few more steps and she'd be free. The glittering light of Nod lay before her, twinkling through the haze like a beacon.

Reaching a hand forward, she could feel the warmth of the sun beginning to rise beyond the shadows, but before she could step through, something cold and hard wrapped around her wrist, pulling her to a stop.

"Catcher of dreams," came a hoarse whisper in the darkness. "Give me your wares."

Azriel closed her eyes, twisting toward the voice. Even the briefest glimpse at a Snarler's eyes could render a Dreamcatcher immobile, turning their flesh to ice.

"Let me go."

A rattling cackle echoed through the mist, and something wet hit her face. "*You* came into *my* realm, catcher."

"I have nothing for you."

The Snarler dragged air into his lungs, letting out a sigh. "Now, now, little one. You dare come into *my* lands and lie to me?" He inhaled again. "We can do this the easy way, or we can do this the hard way. I'll leave it up to you, but either way, I *will* get what I want."

Azriel drew herself up, squaring her shoulders. "I have nothing for you," she repeated, slowly reaching her hand beneath her cape to the curve at the base of her spine. Her fingers met the cool edge of her dagger's hilt, sheathed in a worn leather case strapped around her hips. The blade with an intricately carved bone handle had been in her family for generations. The steel was imbued with the only element known to ward off Snarlers; cadmium.

"Foolish catcher. The hard way it is." He crouched low, his clawed wings spread wide. "There is no escape from the shadow realm without an exchange." His eyes flashed with gold as he pushed up from the ground, leaping towards her.

With nimble fingers, Azriel retrieved the dagger from its scabbard and trusting in her sixth sense alone, she thrust it in the air. Too late the Snarler realised his mistake, and the blade pierced his abdomen as he landed on top of her. A shrill cry escaped his lips, and he rolled to the side.

Azriel pushed up from the ground and ran for the light she could feel pulsing around the edges of Nod. She didn't dare open her eyes, relying solely on her other senses to guide her.

With arms outstretched, she reached for the safety of her homeland. Warmth radiated from her fingertips up to her shoulders, and she squinted her eyes open. The sun sat low in the sky, slowly making its way across the cloudless blue, and Azriel fell to her knees, weeping with joy. She had made it. She was home.

She unhooked her dream net, pushing it before her as she lowered her head and took a deep breath to slow her thundering heart.

"Azriel!" someone called, and she looked up to see her father racing towards her. He waved his arms frantically, and others joined him, their faces twisted into masks of terror.

And then she felt it. The cold cloaking around her ankles and sliding up her legs. She glanced backwards to see she had not made it all the way through the portal. One black wing with an elongated talon at its tip reached through and wrapped around her lower half.

That same rattling cackle echoed through the Land of Nod. Azriel turned to her father with wide eyes before she was dragged back to the shadow realm, the portal snapping shut behind her.

*Dreamcatcher was an instant exercise, where one member gives a prompt – dreamcatcher – and we have five minutes to come up with something. I thought a play on it would be fun. Rather than the threaded wall hangings we know as dreamcatchers, why not have a person who catches dreams?*

*I loved this one so much I decided to extend it past the two and half paragraphs I'd managed to get down before our time was up.*

# Today's the Day

Today's the day I change.
No more standing by.
I've learned my lesson,
I've seen the light.
It's time;
I have to try.
Today's the day I grow.
No more can I be still.
I've made my peace,
I've come this far.
At last
I've found the will.
Today's the day I leave.
No more will I stay.
I've bought a ticket,
I've packed a bag.
And now
I'm going away.
Today's the day I'm free.
No more tears I'll cry.
I've paid the price,
I've done my time.
And so
I say goodbye.

*Today's the Day was inspired by another Reedsy prompt; "Today's the day I change."*

*I had the idea to write from the perspective of someone finding the strength and making a stand to leave their abusive relationship. I see it as a transformative time in one's life; a huge step on their journey from caterpillar to butterfly – making the change they need to survive.*

# Tell me no Lies

"I SWEAR TO GOD, IT'S THE TRUTH!" Joe pulls against his restraints, but it's no use. Even Houdini himself couldn't free himself from the bindings of Virgil St. Clair.

"See, that's not what we heard, was it, boss?" Virgil circles Joe, the toothpick between his teeth flicking side-to-side. "We heard you was in bed with the coppers. Gettin' yourself a nice little pay cheque for informing on some of our acquaintances. Ain't that right, boss?" He sniffs, rubbing his thumb across his nose.

"That's right," comes a voice from the shadows; one that instils fear in men the world over. Marco Demouth is not known for his leniency. He runs a tight ship, and he does not condone deceit of any kind. Especially when it affects his business dealings.

Joe shakes his head. "I didn't do it! I don't even know who Mickey is."

Virgil kicks the legs of the chair out from under him, tipping it backwards. "That's not the way Cassie tells it." He reaches out and drags the blonde woman closer. "You calling her a liar?"

Joe's eyes widen as he glances towards her. He shakes his head vehemently. "No, I would never…"

"Sounds to me like that's exactly what you're doin'," Virgil interrupts. "You're sayin' the boss's daughter didn't tell us it was you?"

"No, I'm not…"

"So you admit it then?"

"No!" Sweat beads on Joe's brow. "I don't deny she told you, or that she heard it, but I'm telling you, it wasn't me. I'm no snitch."

Virgil sucks on the toothpick, shaking his head. "You know how the boss feels about liars, Joe." He drops the woman's arm and stalks into the corner of the room, returning with a can of gasoline.

"W-what are you doing?" Joe fights, struggling against the ropes around his arms and legs. "Please! I swear, it wasn't me!"

Virgil ignores his pleas, unscrewing the cap and tipping the foul-smelling liquid all over Joe's legs, coating his pants. He retrieves a silver lighter from his pocket, flicking the top up and raising a brow. "One last chance."

Tears trail down Joe's cheeks as he begs. "It wasn't me," he whispers, turning his gaze back to Cassie. "Please, tell them…"

"Boss?" Virgil raises a brow in question, but his eyes remain firmly on Joe.

Marco steps out of the shadows, his fingers steepled beneath his chin. "What say you, Cassie? Could you have been mistaken?"

Cassie pulls her lip between her teeth. "I... I don't..." She swallows, taking a step back.

"You don't what, sweetheart?"

Virgil spins the wheel on the lighter, igniting the wick. "Tick, tock."

"Please!" Joe cries out, and the scent of urine permeates the air. "I have a wife and kids at home. Don't do this."

"Cassie?" Marco watches his daughter as she wrings her hands together. "You wouldn't lie to me, would you?"

Her face crumples. "I'm s-sorry," she whispers, burying her face in her hands. "It wasn't him."

The lighter clicks closed, and Joe heaves a sigh of relief, his head falling to his chest.

"You disappoint me." Marco nods at Virgil, and he takes up the can of gasoline. "You leave me no choice." He turns on his heels, leaving the room as the flint catches and her screams ring through the air.

*Tell me no Lies was an assignment titled "Liar, liar, pants on fire." As you can see, I took it quite literally! A little darker than my norm, but it's actually one of my favourites. I wanted to explore the idea of how far a father would go to protect his business, even if it meant the destruction of his family, while also playing on the old rhyme and having the liar's pants literally go up in flames.*

# Time to Wake

A LOUD OBNOXIOUS SOUND, almost like a siren, blears from somewhere nearby. "Shit," a familiar voice hisses, and the sound is silenced. "Goddamn it. Level four on Wednesday."

*Level four?*

I try to speak, but my throat won't cooperate. A raspy gasp of air is all I can manage.

"Steve?" My brother takes my hand, and I turn towards his voice, blinking my eyes against the harsh light streaming through the window behind him. "Jesus, mate, you scared the death out of us."

With a frown, I try again to speak. "Wh-what happened?" I croak.

"Here." Brandon hands me a plastic cup of water. He perches on the bed beside me, and it's then I notice the stark white walls surrounding us, and an incessant beeping sound coming from beside me.

"You're in the hospital. There was an accident. You've been in a coma for six months." Tears fill his eyes. "They told us you might not wake up. It was real touch and go there for a minute."

Another siren goes off down the hall, and Brandon lets out a sigh, raking his hand through his hair. "It's an alert from the government." He waves his phone in the air. "We're going into lockdown in two days' time. No leaving our homes for four weeks."

"What?" I ask. "Why would we be locked in our homes for four weeks? Are we at war?" It could be the splitting headache pounding behind my eyes, but nothing is making sense.

"Nah, nothing like that. Well… not really. The world has turned upside down. Never thought I'd see anything like it in my lifetime. It's like we've stepped back in time to when the plague was around. It's a global pandemic. Coronavirus is what they're calling it." He shakes his head. "They say it's like the flu but spreads faster and is more deadly. It's crazy, man."

I frown, my mind not accepting what he's saying. A global pandemic? How is that possible in this day and age?

The last thing I remember is running through the crowded streets and… a flash of something… a car perhaps, then… everything goes a little hazy. Just an endless stream of fuzz.

"I know, right? It only just came to New Zealand, but we've seen how it went down overseas, so Jacinda's locking it down right off the bat. Wherever you are at midnight on Wednesday, that's where you have to stay for four weeks, unless you're an essential worker."

I can't wrap my head around it. One minute I'm running to catch Sarah before her flight, and… Shit. My eyes widen as I turn to my brother. I'm almost afraid to ask. "Did Sarah…?"

Brandon's face drops and he nods. "Yeah, mate. She got on the plane. Sorry."

Tilting my head back, I close my eyes, willing the endless dream to claim me again. To take me away from this alternate universe I seem to have awoken to. Back to when Sarah was with me, and everything made sense. When the only thing that needed to be locked down was your dinner reservation, not your home.

"It's not all bad, mate," Brandon says with a pat of my leg. "Now that you're awake, you get to come hang out with your big brother for four weeks." He grins, but it doesn't reach his eyes. There's something he's not telling me.

"I lost the house, didn't I?"

"Not entirely." His eyes go all squinty, and he fidgets with the bedsheet over my legs.

"Spill."

Letting out a sigh, he rakes his hand through his hair again. "Don't get mad, but the bank was ready to foreclose seeing as you weren't able to make your mortgage payments, so…" He draws out the word, avoiding my gaze.

"So?" I prompt.

"So, I took over the mortgage." He flings his hands out wide. "I'm your new roomie, bro."

*Time to Wake was written for an assignment where we had to write about a character waking after a six-month coma. A lot can change in six months, and I imagine it would be quite scary to wake and find things are not as you knew them to be. Throw Corona into the mix and going into lockdowns, and you have yourself a waking nightmare.*

# The Roles we Play

MOST OF THEM ARE BLURRED, but a few of the images I managed to salvage from the roll hold me captive. I can't quite believe what I'm seeing. Crowds of people watching a processional down Colombo Street, and there in the foreground, looking directly at the camera, is my brother, his face partially covered by his cap.

"Soooo," Poppy draws out the word, her mouth pulled into a grimace. "What do you think this means?"

"I think it's apparent, isn't it?"

"Is it though? I mean, you can't *really* make out a lot." She squints as if she can't see the glaringly obvious. She can't be so dense as to not have figured it out.

"Look." I point out the familiar open top Rolls Royce driving down the centre of the road in the first shot. There's a man standing in the back, his hand held high in a wave. Beside him is a woman with a large red hat and lace covering her face. Even from this angle it's obvious it's the Prime Minister and First Lady.

"Okay, yeah, but we don't know it's from *that* day though, do we? And he's just standing there."

I shake my head, scrolling to the next image. He's standing back from the crowd, hidden by a cluster of trees. His hand is shoved deep into his pocket.

Poppy reaches out and stays my hand. "Maybe we should stop. We don't need to see any more."

Only I've already seen them. I just needed Poppy to see it too, to make sure my mind isn't playing tricks on me.

I scroll on.

His arm is outstretched, aiming at the vehicle as it passes by.

I click again.

People are running. A lone woman in a trench coat walks away with her head ducked down, and my brother is nowhere to be seen.

Poppy doesn't say anything as she stares at the incriminating image, her shaking hand held to her lips.

I click a button and the screen goes blank, just the shining light of the projector on the white wall.

"What are you going to do?" she whispers, her face now as white as the wall before us.

"I'm handing it in."

"But they'll lock him up. For good."

"I know, and as much as I hate the idea of him being locked up, I have to do this. I can't stand the thought of an innocent man rotting away in prison for the rest of his life, knowing what I do." I turn pleading eyes to her, begging her to understand.

"I can't let you do this."

"Poppy, I know you love him, but we can't just wish it away. Jason did this. He's guilty." I place my hand on her forearm, but she swats me away.

"He was following orders." She pulls her trench coat on and tugs the roll of film from the projector. "And you'd be wise to follow them too."

*The Roles we Play was written for an assignment with the prompt; you find a roll of film; how does the story pan out? It took me right up until the day it was due to come up with something, and I had to rewrite the ending several times before I was happy with it. This one, as you can probably guess, is inspired by the JFK shooting.*

# Laugher is the Best Medicine

Stories and poems that tickle your funny bone.

# Public Relations

"UNBELIEVABLE!" Sarah paces back and forth in front of the table. "It's not at all what I wanted." She waves the newspaper in the air.

"It's not that bad."

She stops, her brows almost jumping from her head. "Not that bad?" She flings the paper down in front of me, her smiling face beaming up at me from the front page. "It's not that good either!"

"It's a lovely photo…"

"I look like a moron! My head is too small for my body, my neck is nigh on invisible, and where did those extra chins come from? Not to mention the bat wings." She pauses, her eyes wide. "Is that what I really look like?" Raising her arm, she pokes at the soft flesh.

"You look happy. And rightly so. It's not every day you get awarded a diploma in…" my eyes flick down as I try to compose myself, "…public relations." When I glance back up, her face is slowly turning crimson.

"See? Even you can't say it with a straight face. She did it on purpose to make me look stupid."

"No, I'm sure it was an accident. They're very similar words to look at."

"Missing the L out of public is *not* an oversight. It's intentional. I should've known Margaret wasn't capable of giving me a good story, what with our history." She drags a hand down her face. "I've been getting calls all day thanks to this fake news."

"Isn't that a good thing?"

"Maybe if they were actually related to my work and not my nether regions. You'd be surprised just how many adults can behave childishly at the mention of the word pubic." Plonking herself down on the couch, she rests her head in her hands. "What am I going to do?"

"I'll tell you what you're going to do. You're going to pull up your big-girl panties and deal with it. This is what you trained for, isn't it? Dealing with the public and reputations? So, go out there and work your magic! Use this fake news to your advantage." I hold my hands out to her, which she accepts. "You can do this, Sarah."

Her teeth clamp onto her bottom lip as she sniffs and blinks away the tears that had been threatening. I can already see the cogs turning as she darts her eyes back and forth.

"Yes." She nods, meeting my gaze. "You're right, this is what I trained for. To hell with Margaret! I'm getting my reputation back!"

*This one was fun to write. Rather than having it be about a story that was untrue (fake news), I wanted it to be a play on words and some sort of rivalry between two people. Once I knew what the diploma was going to be, the rest just fell into place.*

# The Letterbox

IT WAS IN THE LETTERBOX. Just sitting there, staring at me with its multiple creepy eyes, flexing its front legs one at a time, as if about to pounce. The vile creepy crawly had taken up residence in the corner of my letterbox, and it refused to budge. I had a week's worth of mail sitting there, unopened, because every time I opened the damn latch, it came scuttling out to greet me.

The elaborate web seemed to grow larger every day, and my mail appeared to be ensnared.

There was just no way around it. Mr. Arachnid would have to go. But how do you evict an unwanted tenant without having to come into contact? The very thought of those eight hairy legs sent shivers down my spine.

Perhaps I could throw a match and watch the web go up in flames? Or maybe slip the hose nozzle through the slot and blast him out. Both seemed like viable options, yet also flawed.

No. I needed a sure-fire way to end this and blowing him to smithereens seemed like the only real answer.

A stick of dynamite precariously balanced, a long fuse, and a single match. I didn't need that week-old mail anyway.

One… two… three… KABOOM!

The letterbox flew sky-high, and I gave a silent salute of good riddance.

Once the flames had died down, I erected my pretty new letterbox. Standing back to admire my handy work, something in the corner caught my eye. The beginnings of a web, and those creepy little eyes staring back at me.

*I have an aversion for all things creepy crawly, especially spiders. They always seem to take a liking to mailboxes, which can make collecting the mail a nightmare at times. I once had a spider leap out at me when I went to open the box, so when I was given the assignment of "In the letterbox" it was an obvious choice to write about. Only this time I lived out that fantasy of utterly annihilating the blasted thing! Or did I?*

# Rose-tinted glasses

"MORNING," he chirps, as if he didn't just rip my heart out and shove it down my throat. "How did you sleep?"

"Pfft, like you even care," I mutter, clambering out of bed and donning my dressing gown. I can't even bring myself to look at him after what he did, so I brush past him and down the hall to the kitchen. I flick the jug on and stare out the window, contemplating my next move. Susie is out there, of course, picking up her morning paper without a care in the world. Look at her, wearing her fluffy slippers and flannel pyjamas like she owns the place.

"Is everything okay? You seem a little off this morning." Mark comes up behind me, a hand running down my back to rest on my hip.

I snort at his choice of word. I guess I might be a little off… of him, that is. With a shake of my head, I shuffle sideways, out of his grasp, and begin making my coffee. I don't bother offering him one.

"Have I done something wrong?" he asks, his hand rubbing against the coarse stubble on his chin in an irritating way. How have I never noticed how annoying that scratchy sound is before? Have I really been looking at him through those rose-tinted glasses this whole time?

"Because if I have, I don't know what it is." He rests his hip against the bench and watches me with confusion, and I fight the urge to roll my eyes.

"Like you don't know," I spit, turning on my heels and walking away. How can he just sit there acting like everything is fine? It is so not fine. Not by a long shot.

"I really don't know though, Maisy." He grabs my arm and pulls me to face him. "Baby, tell me what I've done so I can fix it." His eyes stare into mine with a sincerity I wasn't expecting. He really has no clue.

But… how is that possible? My brows furrow as I avert my gaze and search for an answer on the wall beside his head. I replay the whole scenario in my mind, and suddenly the angry haze lifts and I'm left feeling foolish. Pulling my lip between my teeth, I turn back to him with a sheepish grin. "I, uh… I had a dream you cheated on me with Susie next door."

"You had a dream?" He pulls back, an odd expression on his face. "Me and Susie?" He points first at himself then out the window towards our neighbour's house. "She's old enough to be my mother."

I nod slowly, my lips pulled to the side. He's right, she is, but it still didn't stop my brain from conjuring up an image of her purple hair in rollers bouncing away on top of my husband last night.

"Just because you're a few years older than me, doesn't mean I'm going to run off with our seventy-year-old neighbour. You know that, right?" He dips his head to meet my gaze with a grin. "You're the only old lady for me."

*As soon as I sat down to write this one, I knew what it was going to be. We've all had those dreams that felt so real that when we wake up, we're not sure if it really happened or not. I'm sure a lot of women out there have also had those dreams that made them angry with their partner too – no matter how irrational that might seem. Dreams can hold a sort of power over us if we let them.*

# Brotherly Love

"COME, COME, BROTHER. It was only a bit of fun." Jordan snickered, drumming his hands on the small table between them. "No harm done."

Lush greenery rolled past the windows either side of them, and grey clouds hung heavy in the air.

"No harm done?" Nathaniel glared, his hands forming fists beneath the table. "We could've been killed."

Jordan held a finger in the air. "Could've, but weren't. Where's your sense of adventure? We're on a train in the highlands of Scotland, brother. Relax a little." He leaned back against his seat, winking at the sultry brunette sitting across the aisle.

"Relax?" Nathaniel shook his head, pointing a finger in his brother's face. "You're the reason we're in this mess in the first place. Don't tell me to relax."

Jordan linked his hands behind his head. "What you call a mess, I call a well-laid plan."

Nathaniel scoffed. "Please enlighten me, dear brother." He waved a hand through the air between them. "What happens next?"

"Well," Jordan leaned forward, his palms pressed against the table. "The conductor is going to come through that door any minute now and ask for our tickets."

"Our non-existent tickets," Nathaniel interjected.

Jordan dismissed his remark with a wave of the hand. "A mere snaffoo in the grand scheme of things." Nathaniel rolled his eyes. "Anyway, that's where you and your muscles come in."

"No."

"Come on, just rough him up a little."

Nathaniel folded his arms. "Not happening. You always do this."

"Do what?"

Nathaniel quirked a brow. "Get us into these impossible messes and expect me to get us out of it."

Jordan smirked, tapping a finger to the tip of his nose. "That's my job as the younger brother. To keep you on your toes." He waggled his brows. "You love it really."

"No, I don't. Just like I didn't like it when you tricked that Scotsman to hitch his kilt up and give me an eyeful of his package." He lowered his voice. "I can't unsee that, Jordan. It'll be forever seared into my retinas."

"Ah, but now you know the answer to the age-old question."

Nathaniel sighed. "And what question is that?"

"What does a Scotsman wear under his kilt, of course." Jordan shook his head, his eyes shining with jest.

"Unlike you, *I* would've lived a content life never knowing the answer to that question. Instead, you've scarred me with a mental image I'd rather not have."

The door behind swooshed open, and a man dressed in a dark suit and hat stepped through. He stopped at each cluster of seats, holding his hand out for tickets.

"You ready?" Jordan grinned, his eyes following the conductor's every move.

"No."

"Here he comes."

"I'm not—"

"Tickets please." His white-gloved hand hung between them, but neither moved. "Tickets." He flapped his fingers in a give-it-here motion.

Jordan patted his jacket and down his body with a look of embarrassment on his face. "I'm sorry, I seem to have misplaced them. Brother?" He raised his brow in challenge.

Nathaniel sighed, his hand wrapping around the conductor's throat and slamming his face into the table. "This is the last time, *brother*."

*Brotherly Love was a combination of two assignments – A train journey, and a mischievous trickster. I was inspired by the one and only Loki from the Marvel universe, and I used a train ride through Scotland as my scene as my Jacobite train journey was still fresh in my memory from my trip to the UK back when the world was still open to travel.*

# Corona

"PLEASE TELL ME YOU HAVEN'T been sitting there all morning." Alfie sighs as he sits across from his wife. A slight twitch to her lips is the only sign she's heard him, but she doesn't move from her spot. Her forgotten coffee sits on its coaster where he placed it two hours earlier. "Have you at least eaten, love?"

She snorts, turning two beady eyes towards him. "Who can eat at a time like this?" She turns back to the window, her nose mere centimetres from the glass.

Alfie clears his throat, shuffling his seat closer and sliding a hand across the table. "I know this whole lockdown thing is a little scary, but we don't have to stay indoors. How about we go outside? Have a little walk around the streets? I hear people are putting teddy-bears up in the neighbourhood for the kids to find. Why don't we see if we can spot them?" His fingers brush against her elbow, and she glares at him.

"Go out there? With all of *them*?" she demands. "You're out of your mind, Alfie. You haven't seen what they've been doing out there. It's madness!" She tugs at the binoculars hanging around her neck. "This corona-whatsit is doing things to their minds." She taps her forehead. "Making them crazy."

"I don't think it works that way, love. People are just doing what they can to keep the boredom at bay."

Agnes tuts, pulling the binoculars from her neck and handing them to Alfie. "Just you look." She points out the window. "Across there. That woman has been out in her front yard in at least ten different outfits since this morning. Ten, Alfie! She's been jumping in and out of bushes, rolling around on the ground, talking to herself." She shakes her head. "Poor thing is falling apart."

"I don't know," Alfie says as he holds the binoculars to his eyes. "She doesn't look crazy to me. Maybe she's making one of those tic-tac things the news was talking about the other night. Some new video thing the young ones are doing."

"Don't be so silly, Alfie. She's lost the plot. She has the corona."

"Well, look over there." He points to a couple in matching tracksuits, walking briskly down the street. "They look perfectly normal to me, and they're outside in the fresh air. Look, they even waved at her." He turns to his wife with a smile. "It can't be that bad out there."

She huffs and rolls her eyes. "They've been past three times already today. They don't stop, Alfie. They just keep walking around and around. I'm telling you. The people in this neighbourhood are going downhill fast. I'm not going out there and letting it get me too." She folds her arms across her chest, shaking her head. "No, thank you."

"It can't get you unless you're in contact with someone who's sick though, Agnes."

"That's what they want you to think! I've been listening though. It's those microwaves or some such. We're all just breathing it in, and then it takes over your brain." She waves her hand towards the window. A man clad in Lycra bends and stretches. "See? It's just not natural, Alfie. Who in their right mind would do that?"

"I think they're just trying to get fit, love."

"Hogswash. No one exercises of their own free will. I'm telling you, Alfie, it's not normal." She takes up the binoculars and turns back to the window. "That's why we have to stay vigilant and keep watch. That corona won't get past me. You can bet on it."

*Corona was an assignment called "In this neighbourhood", and I instantly thought of the goings on while everyone was in lockdown when Covid first hit.*

*TikTok had become more popular, and there were a lot of people out and about more frequently for those busybody neighbours to keep an eye on.*

# Two Pink Lines

MY HEAD POUNDS as I stare at the two pink lines in despair. What am I going to tell my parents? What am I going to tell my teachers? What am I going to do?

I knew it was a mistake to go out with my friends on a school night. I don't do things like that. I'm a good girl. I stay home and study, preparing for University. At least, that's what I used to do until I met Sam a few months back. Suddenly homework and cramming for midterms didn't seem so important anymore.

It started off innocently; a Big Mac combo and a movie, then onto cruising up and down the main street in lowered cars with noisy exhausts. And then it wasn't long before I started being invited to parties, and even though I've never been much of a party girl, I went along with it because Sam was going, and I desperately wanted to be anywhere he was.

I was falling for him. Hard.

At first, I stayed sober, not wanting to partake in the drinking, but Sam was having one, so I figured why not? One won't hurt.

One drink turned into two, turned into six.

Blurred vision, making out, frenzied dancing to techno music, deep and meaningful conversations about the inner workings of the universe, and then stumbling home in the dark. Stifling my drunken giggles as I tried to sneak through the veggie garden so my parents wouldn't hear me. Forgetting about the irrigation pipes strewn through said garden and catching my foot. Losing what little balance I had left as I plummeted face first into the wrought-iron gate that separated the garden from the house.

And now, here I am, on school photo day, with two lines that resemble bright pink judder bars on my forehead.

*Two Pink Lines was an assignment where we had to write about a mistake. I thought it would be fun to write a story that was different to what it seemed.*

# Happy Thoughts

"MY MARBLES. Have you seen them?" Tootles asked as he tossed another cushion across the room. "I've searched everywhere, and I can't find them." He sniffled, swiping an angry hand across his eyes. "I could've sworn I left them right there." He pointed at the tree stump in the centre of the room. They used this as a table when playing cards in the evenings.

"Sorry, Tootles, I haven't seen them. But I can help you look," Wendy offered, dropping to her knees and peering beneath the worn armchair in the corner.

"Thanks, Wendy." His voice waivered, overcome with grief. "I can't fly without them." A sob burst from his lips, and he buried his face in his hands.

"Oh, Tootles," Wendy gushed, rushing over to wrap him in her arms. "Whatever do you mean? Marbles can't make you fly." She frowned, realising it was no sillier to believe in the fairy dust they all used. After all, this was Neverland, and anything was possible.

Tootles pulled away from her embrace, resting on his haunches. "But they *do*, Wendy. *Mine* do." His lips twisted to the side. "They're where I keep my happy thoughts."

"Oh." That was a problem then. You needed fairy dust *and* happy thoughts to fly. "But can't you think of

some new happy thoughts?" She scoured the room then quickly snatched up a tiny pebble. "You could think of one thing right now and store it in here." She smiled, holding her hand out flat with the pebble on her palm.

Tootles frowned. "You can't keep happy thoughts in a stone, Wendy." His tone suggested it was a ridiculous notion.

Her hand fell to her lap, the pebble rolling to the floor. As she stooped to pick it up, she caught sight of something glinting.

"Wait a second…" Lying flat on her stomach, she wiggled beneath the couch, all the way to the back. A fluffy bear and a dirty sock were tucked away in the corner, and there, poking out from behind the bear's bottom, was a marble. She plucked it out and sent it rolling towards Tootles, followed by four more.

"Oh, Wendy!" he exclaimed, jumping to his feet. "You found them! You found my happy thoughts!"

As she shimmied her way back out, Tootles leapt into the air, his eyes closed, and his hand held in a tight fist. He zoomed to the ceiling and did a circuit of the room before landing down beside her. "Thank you, Wendy. Thank you for finding my marbles."

Happy Thoughts *was written for an assignment where we were to start a story with a character who has lost something important to them.* Peter Pan *is a favourite childhood story, and I adored the movie adaptation,* Hook. *Of course, as soon as I heard the assignment, I instantly thought of Tootles and his missing marbles.*

# Uninvited

"WHAT DO YOU THINK OF PURPLE? Or maybe pink?" I ask, fluffing my hair with my hand. "I've always wanted to try those colours."

"Ooh, you'd really suit purple. Do you want me to help? I'm actually qualified, would you believe?" Tabitha chuckles, zipping up her suitcase and extending the handle. She pulls it along behind her as we walk towards her car.

"You are? What are you doing here then?" I wave my hand at the Nail Tech building we just left.

"I want a salon that offers both hair and nails." She grins. "It's all part of my master plan."

"Of course. I forgot about that." The first day of class, Tabitha had sat at the table beside me, introduced herself, and then proceeded to explain her five-year plan. I had been suitably impressed. Four years my junior, and she has her whole life planned out, while I can barely manage to plan my meals for the week, let along my next five years.

"I might even have some purple dye at home. You should come over this weekend." She tugs at the hair hanging around my face. "I've been dying to get my hands on these greys since day one." She grins, stopping at her car. "Come around tomorrow morning, okay? And bring that hunky boyfriend of yours."

I nod, waving my hand, when inside I'm still trying to process what she said.

She's been dying to get her hands on my *greys*? My hand moves to my hair. What greys? I'm only 26. I don't have grey hair!

I climb into my car and pull onto the road. My eyes keep flicking up to the rearview mirror, trying to catch a glimpse of the greys she's talking about, but all I see is blonde.

Back at home, I switch the light in the bathroom on and peer at my reflection. I twist side-to-side, and there, above my ear, is a thick strand of silver hair. And another farther back on my head, and even more towards my temple. In fact, there are loads of them slotted in between the fine blonde strands.

I stare in horror as my fingers pull out more and more of the offending strands. When did this happen? How long have they been there? I don't remember inviting these intruders onto my head. I'm not even thirty yet!

I bet it started when Tabitha noticed Darryl, my boyfriend, one afternoon after class. He'd come to pick me up, and the next morning, Tabitha had practically frothed at the mouth telling me how hot he was. It had been a little disturbing, but I'd put it behind me and moved on, even forming a friendship of sorts with her. But now… Now I had grey hairs to thank her for. And she had the audacity to point them out to me.

Bracing my hands on the sink, I gape at the coarse hairs I've gathered, and another unpleasant thought occurs to me. Pulling my lips between my teeth, I step back from the sink, grab hold of my waistband, and pull it away from me. The elastic pings against my skin as my fingers lose grip and I stumble backwards. "No," I whisper. "No, no, no." This can't be happening.

With tweezers in hand, I tug the fabric of my pants down again and pluck the shining hair from my nether regions. I add it to the pile of hairs in the sink and turn the tap on, washing away all evidence of my uninvited guests.

Uninvited *was an assignment titled "the uninvited guest", and though it's not where most people's mind would instantly go, mine went to a particular memory of mine from when I was training to be a nail technician. One of the girls in class had continually told me how attractive my fiancé was, and then proceeded to tell me how she wanted to attack my greys, which I was completely oblivious to. Thus,* Uninvited *was born.*

# Out of my Depth

Still no boats or signs of rescue.
My help sign washed away again
last night. I have no energy
to put up a new one.
I'm so hungry. I've been dreaming of a juicy
piece of fish, and I've decided
I have no other options left.
My spear is sharp enough now.
I'm going to try it. Once the sun is high,
and the tide is out, I'm going fishing
in the shark-infested waters.

They're only babies. What harm could they do?

We were given the assignment Day 52 on a desert island, and at first, I was stumped on how to go about this, but then it hit me. I grabbed a piece of paper, crumpled it up, dabbed tea on it and dripped red nail-polish over it, then wrote this short piece here.

# Too Good to be True

SARAH PULLED UP OUTSIDE the log cabin nestled in amongst the luscious trees of every shade of green. The nearest town was ten kilometres away, and there were no other houses in sight. She was truly alone. It was almost too good to be true. After the year she'd had, she just wanted some time to herself to regroup and figure out what to do next.

When she'd begun looking into accommodation, most places were out of her budget, but then this little beauty had seemingly fallen into her lap. An ad on Facebook had lured her in with its picturesque charm, and the price had been far less than anything else she'd come across.

She unfurled herself from the car, stretching her arms above her head before retrieving her bag from the back seat and heading inside. The kitchen was quaint; pot belly stove, copper pots hanging above the island in the centre, and a small bay window with planters full of herbs.

The living area was cosy and warm, a roaring fire already burning to take the chill off. She dropped her bag and flopped down on the worn couch, draping herself in the blanket hanging on the back. The drive had been long, and she was exhausted. She'd close her eyes for just a few moments before unpacking and getting properly settled.

Music filled her ears, soft and soothing. She didn't remember switching the radio on, but perhaps it was on a timer. Either way, it was nice. Beethoven maybe? Mozart? She never could tell the difference. The smell of fresh coffee tickled her nostrils. Must be on a timer as well.

She peeled her eyes open, a yawn catching her by surprise. She sat up, twisting her neck side-to-side, and leapt from her seat. "Who are you?" she demanded of the man sitting at the kitchen bench with his hands wrapped around a mug.

"I was going to ask you the same question, but you looked so peaceful, I didn't want to wake you." He smiled, holding his mug up. "Coffee? I just made a pot."

Sarah clutched the blanket to her chest, as if it could shield her from him. "What are you doing here?"

He grabbed another mug and poured the enticing black liquid in. "Sugar? Milk?"

She nodded, waiting him out.

He walked over to the couch, placing her steaming mug on the coffee table. "Here you go." He sat down opposite her. "I'm Mike, and you are?" He held his hand out.

She eyed him warily before accepting his hand. It was rough and calloused. "Sarah," she said.

"You saw the ad on Facebook too, huh?"

Her eyes widened. How could he know that?

He shook his head, chuckling. "I knew there had to be a catch."

"What do you mean?" She frowned.

"The price was ridiculous. I mean, look at this place." He waved his arm around the room, and Sarah took the place in again with fresh eyes. "It was foolish to think anyone would charge so little for it."

He was right. She'd known it when she pulled up, and she knew it now upon further inspection. They'd been set up.

She dropped the blanket to the floor, rubbing a hand down her face. "So you booked to stay here, and so did I," she clarified.

"Looks like it." Mike stretched his arms across the back of the couch. "I hope you don't snore."

Sarah opened her mouth to retort when the sound of gravel crunching beneath tyres caught her attention. She peered out the window behind her to see a cloud of dust moving towards them. She turned back to Mike with wide eyes.

"Guess we're not the only ones who answered the ad," he said, heading back to the kitchen and pouring a coffee for the newcomer.

"Um, I haven't had a chance to look around the place yet," I said. "Just how many rooms are there?"

"Four." He grinned. "Looks like we're having a party."

*Too Good to be True* was an assignment where we had to write about a bargain vacation with a stranger in a shared cabin. A bit of an odd one, and rather specific, but it was fun. I have added a little onto the end of this one, as our assignments are meant to be 500 words, and I had only just uncovered that they'd both rented the same place at that point. I love the idea of someone secretly renting out rooms to strangers.

# Stunned Mullet

"WHAT'LL IT BE, DOLL?" The perky blonde chews her gum loudly as she fastens a cape around my neck.

My fingers twitch, reaching for the silk scarf I'd tied around my head before walking out the door. The same one I'd been wearing the past week.

I meet her eyes in the mirror, and she gives me an encouraging smile. Huffing out a sigh, I slowly tug the scarf free, letting it fall to the floor, and behind me, the hairdresser stifles a gasp.

It's bad. I know it is.

Swallowing the lump in my throat, I raise my mournful eyes to hers. "Can you fix it? Please tell me you can fix it."

She clicks her tongue, her nimble fingers tugging at the short tufts on top and the longer sections at the back.

I don't know what came over me. It had seemed like such a good idea at the time; God only knows why.

I'd been scrolling reel after reel of people giving themselves cute dos and they made it look so easy. Something even I, the girl who has not a creative bone in her body, could manage. Alas, my scissors had other ideas.

After the first snip, I knew I'd made a mistake and tried to rectify it by cutting the other side to even it up. It only made things worse. Again and again I tried, snipping one piece here and another there, trying desperately to fix my error, but it was too late. Before I knew it, I was sitting on the floor, surrounded by the massacre of my once gorgeous locks, tears streaming down my face as I gulped back a wine and stared at what appeared to be something akin to the 'business in the front, party in the back' style of the 80s. Only, my business looked more like it'd been attacked by a lawnmower.

That was a week ago, and I hadn't stepped foot out the door since.

"Well?" I peer up at her with hopeful eyes. "Is it salvageable?"

She grins, taking hold of my shoulders. "Of course, hon. This ain't my first lockdown lop off."

*I'd been struggling to write after a year of pushing myself to release a record number of books, and for whatever reason, this assignment (bad hair day) was the first thing I'd written and felt good about in months.*

*There are photos of me as a youngster with a hideous haircut, much like the one I described, though it was intentional back then. It was the 80s and acceptable then! But that, along with the memory of me cutting my hair short during lockdown, was what I based this story on. Luckily, my DIY haircut didn't turn out as bad as the poor woman in my story!*

# A Date with Disaster

"OF COURSE, YOU KNOW, he's one of those lizard people, so you've gotta—"

"I'm gonna stop you right there," I say, holding my palm up. "Um, what? Lizard people?"

Stuart leans back in his seat with a smarmy smirk on his face that just makes me want to punch him. "You don't know about the lizard people?"

"Uh, no, can't say that I do." But I'm sure I'm about to find out.

He runs his tongue along his top teeth as he glances around the room before shuffling his seat forward and piercing me with an almost deranged stare. "Buckle in, baby. I'm about to blow your mind."

I wish someone would blow my mind right now. Blow it right out of this dinky restaurant, if it can even be called that, and straight back to my sofa with a drink of Jamesons and a slice of pizza. At least I could flick through Netflix to keep entertained instead of listening to whatever conspiracy theory this guy is on about. I should've known it was going to be an epic fail the moment I saw his screen name; BigDaddy69. Only a douchebag would come up with that. Or someone overcompensating for something.

Either way, there most definitely will not be a second date. Hell, I can barely stay awake for the one I'm currently in.

"…and that's why you know old Bill has gotta be one of them, because he's planting shit in our brains…"

Oh Jesus, this one is off the rails. What the hell did I get myself into?

"…haven't you ever noticed how the ads are customised to suit you?" He taps his forehead. "They're always listening, watching, learning." He leans back again, folding his arms. "Subliminal messages, man."

"Right." I draw out the word as I signal to the waiter. I'm going to need a lot more alcohol to deal with this maniac. "So, when I go on the book of faces and see an ad for a unicorn onesie, that's the lizard people brainwashing me, is it?"

Stuart nods, his eyes glinting as if I've somehow agreed with the horseshit streaming from his mouth.

"And what exactly is that going to achieve? If I buy said onesie?"

"It's all about compliance. They plant seeds inside your brain and make you think it was your idea. They're building up to something bigger." He holds his hands up, a metre apart. "And old Bill's not the only one, either." He waggles his brows, bracing his hands on the table. "I heard they've infiltrated all the major governments around the globe, including here. That's how they'll eventually take over."

"Let me get this straight, you think Cindy is a lizard in disguise?"

"Oh no." He shakes his head. "Not her. But the opposition…" He widens his eyes and nods. "She most definitely is. In fact, I wouldn't be surprised if the whole party is in on it."

"The whole of the National party are lizards trying to take over the country?"

He drums his fingers on the table. "Exactly."

Jesus, Mary, and Joseph. I watch him take a swig of his drink, swiping the back of his hand across his wet lips with a grin, and I can't help but wonder exactly how much of the Kool-Aid this guy has been drinking. He's probably one of those guys who thinks there was no moon landing either, or that Elvis is still alive and kicking.

"Can I ask you something?" He looks at me expectantly, so I nod. It can't be any worse than the current topic of conversation. "What do you really think they're hiding in Area 51?"

I stand corrected.

"Because I think it's the hibernation tank for the lizard people. You know, where they implant their lizard foetuses into fertile human women."

My eyes widen as I inadvertently suck in a breath while at the same time taking a sip of my drink. A cough erupts from deep in my chest, and I fight to place the glass down on the table while my body convulses, trying to rid my lungs of the Jamesons and ginger ale they have inhaled.

"Are you alright?" he asks, glancing sidewards, as if *I'm* the embarrassing one.

"I'm fine," I choke out, thumping a hand into my chest. A waitress stops by the table, offering a glass of water, and I accept with a forced smile. "I'm good." I drag in another shaky breath, my eyes wet with the unshed tears that form when your life flashes before your eyes. I thump another hand to my chest, letting out another barking cough.

Stuart frowns at me, his lips pulled to the side as if he's trying to work me out. His eyes seem to dart about my face, and his lips quiver as he speaks to himself under his breath. Then his eyes widen, and he pushes back from the table, a finger pointed in my direction. "I know what you are!"

"Excuse me?" I dab a napkin beneath my eyes.

"You're one of them," he hisses.

I sigh, leaning my elbows on the table. "One of who?"

"The lizard people!" He doesn't even try to hide the idiocy coming from his mouth. "I'm right, aren't I? That's why you reacted that way. Area 51 is where it's all happening." He shakes his head, muttering to himself.

Is it too much to ask that I find a decent guy and *not* one who probably lives in his parents' basement making hats out of tinfoil? Because I know that's what this guy is normally doing on a Friday night. I'm probably the only person desperate enough to have swiped right on him. I won't make that mistake again.

I'm ready to call it a night. I gave it my best shot, but this date needs to end, now. There's only one way to do this. I raise my bare wrist to my lips, whispering, "He's onto me. He knows too much."

His eyes flick up to me, widening, and he swallows audibly. "Wh-who are you talking to? Who is that?" he demands, pointing at my arm.

I glance up at him and nod. "Roger that. Protocol Alpha?"

His face turns white and a sheen of perspiration hangs on his top lip. "P-protocol Alpha?"

I turn my body to the side. "Elimination? Are you sure?" I make a point of peering over my shoulder at him. "If you say so." Pressing my thumb to my wrist, I clear my throat and stand, tugging at the hem of my top before swivelling to face the now empty table and the retreating back of Stuart. With a chuckle, I sit back down and grab my glass, downing it in one. Raising my hand, I signal to the waitress. "Can you have our meals boxed up to go please? Change of plans." I plaster on a smile.

She eyes the vacant seat opposite me. "Both of them?"

"Sure, why the hell not? May as well get something good out of this date."

Her brows arch and she nods with a knowing smile. "We've all been there."

I laugh, crunching on an ice cube. "I very much doubt it."

*I was listening to a podcast a while back, and they were talking about conspiracy theories. I was so captivated by the crazy stories they believed, and it made me think how that would play out in a dating situation. I wasn't sure where I was going to go with it, and I had toyed with the idea of turning it into something full length, but so far, it hasn't gone any further. I did use it for an assignment about a first date though.*

# Season's Greetings

Stories and poems about the holiday season.

# Holiday Cheer

It's my favourite time of the year.

A time for joy and spreading cheer.

A time for spending with those we love,

And remembering those up above.

A time for indulging in sweet treats,

And devouring tasty eats.

A time for drinking a wine or three,

Or perhaps a hot toddy.

A time for sharing lots of laughter

To remember forever after.

# Christmas Fun

Twas the week before Christmas, and all through the town,
Wallets once bulging, were now flattened down.

A second mortgage taken, and a loan for your soul,
Just so you can buy that Swarovski bowl.

It takes pride of place on your table so fancy,
All to outdo your nemesis, Nancy.

There's glitter and tinsel, and baubles galore,
And even a wreath adorning your door.

But Nancy has reindeer, a sleigh, and some canes.
Her house is lit up like a runway for planes.

So, back to the store you trudge all a wary,
To find one more thing, perhaps a gold fairy?

You make your way home with arms overflowing,
To one-up your neighbour by making it snowy.

You aim the machine at your lawn all aglow,
And slowly start spreading a layer of snow.

But the trigger gets stuck, and the sprayer won't stop.
And snow fires out at one hundred knots.

It covers the windows, the gardens and deck.
And still it keeps going, till you cry, "Bloomin'
'eck!"

And Nancy comes running to see what's the matter.
To see why you're making a terrible clatter.

She grabs for the gun, and you wrestle together
To wrangle the weapon that's causing this weather.

It comes to a stop with a godawful splutter,
But not before filling up all of the gutters.

You turn to Nancy with eyes open wide,
As you notice the chaos has spread to her side.

You've gone overboard. You had such a nerve.
So you brace for the scolding you rightly deserve.

But Nancy just smiles and her shoulders she shrugs,
And then she starts laughing and gives you a hug!

"Merry Christmas," she says as she waves her
goodbye,
Heading back to her home with a glint in her eye.

And you watch with confusion, a frown on your face.
Could it be that this whole thing was never a race?

There was no competition, no fight with dear Nancy.
She really just wanted her house to look fancy.

It was all in your head, a game for the season,
That you made into a fight, with no rhyme and no
reason.

# Who is Santa?

Tis the eve of Christmas, a day full of glee,
When children awake to gifts under the tree.

I ready the reindeer and check over the sleigh,
It's nearing the time when we must be away.

The elves are still building, their fingers so nimble,
Painting a scene on the head of a thimble.

When out of the workshop, a scooter rolls free,
And without any warning, it flies into me.

I land with a thud on the snow-covered ground,
My head hits the sleigh, and it's starting to pound.

My eyes flutter closed as darkness unfolds,
But I'm shaken awake by someone in gold.

"You have to get up," he says with a frown.
"Now's not the time to be lying down.

"Children are sleeping and counting on you.
You have to get up, there's so much to do."

I climb to my feet with my head in my hands,
And that's when I realise, I know not of these lands.

"Where am I?" I ask. "And what do you mean?"
This place is not like any other I've seen.

"You're Santa," he says. "Good ol' Saint Nick.
And you need to get moving, quicker than quick."

He points to the reindeer then to a sleigh.
"It's time to get in. You must be on your way."

"You must be confused. I can't be Saint Nick.
I'm just a man, and I have no magic."

Clicking my fingers to show that he's wrong,
I'm shocked when the sleigh starts to belt a familiar
song.

"You are him," he says, "and there's no time to dally.
Your first stop is Dallas, and her name is Sally."

He gives me a push and encouraging smile.
The guy is quite clearly stuck in denial.

"I don't even know how to get there," I say.
"Just climb in," he says. "They know the way."

He points to the reindeer that stamp at the snow,
And for whatever reason, I cannot say no.

I climb into the sleigh all loaded with toys,
To deliver to all of the girls and the boys.

I tug on the reins but don't get very far.
At this point it's probably faster by car.

A memory unfurls of stories we told,
And deep in my mind, it starts to unfold…

"On Holly, on Jolly, on Folly," I try.
But they don't move a muscle, no blink of the eye.

"On Cherry, and Mary, on Jerry and Ben.
On Gertie, and Mertyl, and is one of them Glen?"

Still nothing happens, no reindeer take flight.
How will we do this in only one night?

I squeeze my eyes shut and try to remember,
The stories and songs we heard every December.

Something unravels and starts to take shape.
I open my eyes, my mouth all agape.

"On Dasher, and Dancer, on Prancer, and Vixen.
On Comet, and Cupid, on Donner, and Blitzen."

Then all of a sudden, we're up in the air,
And down below us the elves start to cheer.

We dip and we dive through a flutter of snow

And out of my mouth bursts a "Ho, Ho, Ho, Ho!"

*Every year we have a Christmas get together, and we usually have to write a Christmas poem. This time they decided to make it easier on those who aren't fond of poetry and gave us the option to write a story or poem using the words Holly, Jolly, and Folly.*
*It took me a while to come up with a way to use those words, but then it came to me while watching* The Santa Clause *one night. A Santa who has forgotten he's Santa and has to remember who he is and how he does what he does.*

# A Note From the Author

Thank you so much for reading my collection of stories and poems. I hope you enjoyed them!

As always, I have to thank TRINA for her super proofing talents! Thank you for checking I've crossed the T's and dotted the I's.

To the ASHBURTON WRITERS' GROUP for challenging me to try new things and supporting me in everything I do. I love you guys!

Last but certainly not least, to all the READERS out there who're taking a chance on me and my stories. Without you I couldn't do what I love so much. Thank you!

# Other Books by Stacey Broadbent

**Standalone**
*Never Judge a Book*
*Emma*
*Deep Heat*
*Lady Luck: A Deep Heat bonus novella*
*Fever*
*A Christmas Tail*
*Broken*
*Awesome Applesauce*

**A Step in Time series**
*Dancing through the Storm*
*Dancing in Circles*
*Dancing with Destiny*
*A Step in Time: the complete series*

**Super Mum series**
*Frazzled*
*Frazzled and Frumpy*
*Frazzled, Frumpy and Fabulous!*
*Super Mum: the complete series*

**Dark sins novellas**
*Sins of the Flesh*
*Mine*

## Hellhounds MC

*Cut Loose*
*Break Loose*
*Let Loose (coming soon)*

## Musings of a Writer

*Musings, Mournings, and Misadventures*
*Musings, Mayhem, and Mystery*
*Musings, Magic, and Mischief*
*Musings of a Writer: the complete collection*

## Anthologies

*Scars to your Beautiful*
*Witching Hour: Vices and Virtues*
*The White Ribbon Collection*
*Key to my Heart*
*A Touch of Inspiration*
*No Place Like Home*
*Serendipity*
*Lucky Star*
*Hellhounds*

# About the Author

Stacey Broadbent is a multi-genre author from New Zealand. She writes under three different names and a variety of genres, so there is something to suit most tastes. You can find her LGBTQIA reads under the name Cyan Tayse, and children's books under the name Stacey Jayne.

An avid reader and lover of all things bookish, Stacey has made it her goal to share about her favourite authors and books she's read, while also building her own publishing story. She is a qualified proofreader and is embarking on a new journey of study - Library and Information Skills.

She is a member of the Unhinged Kiwi Booktalk discord group, and a great bunch of Canterbury based bookstagrammers. Her TBR is never-ending, and though she struggles to keep up with it, she continues to add more.

As well as reading, her hobbies include LEGO, cross-stitch, crochet, and diamond art, and you can often find her sharing about her latest project on TikTok.

If you feel like stalking her, here are the links!

www.staceybroadbent.com/
www.facebook.com/StaceyBroadbentAuthor
www.amazon.com/author/staceybroadbent
Goodreads: https://goo.gl/YJ6dXa
www.instagram.com/authorstaceybroadbent/
www.bookbub.com/authors/stacey-broadbent
www.tiktok.com/@authorstaceybroadbent